RAPTURE

For Jessica —

JESSICA MARTING

Thank you for reading !

SHADOW PRESS

RAPTURE

Rapture

Second Edition

ISBN 978-1-989780-21-3

Copyright © 2017, 2023 by J.L. Turner

Cover art by German Creative

RAPTURE was previously published by Evernight Publishing.

CONTENT WARNING:

Parental emotional and physical abuse; family estrangement; torture and mutilation.

For Mum, my biggest supporter.

CHAPTER 1

It was well past the time Kai thought he would be home when he left that evening. It took a moment for him to remember that no one was inside the house, waiting in the dark to yell at him for stumbling in during the wee hours of the morning.

He was married now. He didn't have to answer to anyone.

To his surprise, marriage had bought him the closest thing he'd ever known to freedom. He probably should have stopped resisting it years ago. By Ralani standards, eighteen years old was long past the time to throw in the towel and embrace matrimony. While he and his wife weren't exactly embracing it, at least he didn't have to deal with his parents' rules anymore. He and Brya had their own small but well-appointed house on the edge of Hellar, Ralani's capital city.

Kai had reveled until a bouncer kicked him out of his current favorite underground club for being excessively intoxicated. "Excessively intoxicated," he muttered to himself as he trundled along. "Is there any other kind of intoxication?"

He was a little nervous now, walking through the Hellar's dark streets at this ungodly hour, the sound of his boots' leather soles against the uneven cobblestones far too loud in the silence. He could hardly tell if one or more of the shadowy figures lurking in alleys and corners would recognize the deeply flawed only son of the House of Gref and take advantage of his lack of sobriety.

Kai stumbled up the pair of stairs that led to the front door of his house, a wedding gift from his parents. He tried to place his hand in the door's palm lock but could swear the damn thing kept moving. He was finally able to let himself into the darkened house and didn't turn on the lights on the off-chance Brya was home and sleeping. He doubted she would be there, though. Since their marriage, she had returned to the arms of the boyfriend she'd had since she was fifteen. Arranged marriage be damned, Brya was *not* giving up the man she had deemed the love of her life. Kai had agreed to that prior to their marriage, and had been searching for a lady friend of his own since the wedding. He hadn't been successful thus far.

A quick check of the small house's rooms confirmed Brya wasn't home. Kai went to the kitchen and boiled a pot of coffee, an indulgence that drove both of their families up the wall. Coffee wasn't native to Ralani, and it was one of his preferences that his parents routinely railed against. He could practically hear them complaining at him, their voices rusty from disuse, about what he found so wrong about good, strong Ralanian tea as he waited for the water to boil.

What was wrong with acknowledging the time they were living in and embracing the universe outside Ralani? Kai and Brya both hated cooking and had discussed ways to smuggle in a replicator courtesy of her off-world contacts. Kai liked those conversations. They made him feel like he and his wife were friends, almost a real couple.

But they weren't a couple and never would be. Their entire marriage was a political strategy on the parts of their parents. Everyone involved was mortified their only children actually had to physically speak to be heard. Marrying them off to one another and tossing them in this small house had been convenient for everyone. At least Kai would no longer be obligated to serve on Ralani's high council anymore, which would have caused further embarrassment to his parents. And he could physically speak with Brya without receiving glares from people who communicated solely via telepathy.

Kai savored a cup of coffee and sighed at the jigsaw puzzle spread across the kitchen table, one of Brya's pastimes. He picked up a couple of loose pieces, then forced his eyes to focus. He snapped one of them into place.

The front door slamming open knocked him out of his thoughts. A scream rent through the house and Kai spilled some coffee on the puzzle pieces. He got up from the table and stumbled a little, bracing himself against the tabletop.

"Stop!" He heard Brya's cry from the foyer and moved as quickly as he could to the source.

"Brya?" His voice came out a croak. He cleared his throat and tried again. "Brya?"

Standing in the doorway was his mother-in-law, the formidable wife of the High Eminent Authority Fourth Seat on the High Council. Fika Dennir terrified both of them, and she filled the foyer, towering over Brya. She raised her hand and struck her again, clipping the side of her daughter's hands with her long fingernails.

The sight sobered him up far more than the coffee had. "What the *fuck*?" Kai shouted. "Fika, what are you doing?" He hurried to Brya and held out a hand to help her up, but Fika pushed him away. Kai hit the wall and sank to the floor.

"Don't do anything," Brya said through her sobs. "You'll make it worse."

"Kai, Brya tells me you knew about her lover," Fika spat. "And you did *nothing*."

Fear knotted in the pit of his stomach. He couldn't form a response. How did one tell their mother-in-law about the unorthodox agreements that kept a marriage working? Why was it any of her concern, anyhow? They weren't expected to produce non-telepathic children and add to their families' humiliation.

Fika's voice rose. Her speech was garbled and hurried, betraying that she hardly ever spoke the physical, inferior way. She grabbed Brya's arm and half lifted her off the floor. "This is the worst thing either of you have ever done!" she screamed. "First, you can't communicate like the rest of us. Then my daughter—your wife!—runs around in the night like a whore!" She pushed away Brya and planted a kick in her midsection for good measure before moving on to Kai. She launched herself at him, pinning him to the wall and raining blows wherever his hands couldn't protect himself. Brya screamed again, a heartrending sound that had Kai reaching for her, but he was rebuffed when Fika pushed him away.

Fika had stopped her tirade, but Kai knew from her expression that she had simply stopped trying to talk and was now cursing them in her mind. There was a red haze clouding above her head, roiling like a storm cloud from hell.

With a shock, Kai realized he was seeing an aura for the first time in his life, and was sickened to see it turn dark gray with rage, the color of spoiled meat.

With a final roar, Fika slammed his head against the foyer wall, and everything went dark.

———

He came to groggily, to the sounds of Brya weeping and begging him to open his eyes. She was cradling his head in her hands, squeezing tears out of swollen eyes. Early dawn light dappled the floor courtesy of Ralani's three suns. How long had he been out?

"Thank the gods!" she gasped when his eyes fluttered open. "Kai, we have to get out of here."

"We're at home," he muttered. More sleep sounded good about now. He had a hell of a headache, not all of it because of a hangover. "What time is it?"

"It's half past four in the morning, and we have to leave Ralani," she said. "My mother is on a rampage, and soon your parents will be. She attacked Dav this morning, too." Her boyfriend. The person Kai would never admit to anyone in a million years he was jealous of.

"The fuck—why'd she go after Dav?"

"Because she's pissed off and she's crazy like everyone else on this fucking planet. I already packed bags for us. We have to go, *now*. Dav booked us seats on a freighter." She stood up, yanking on his hands until he forced himself to his feet.

"We can't travel on a freighter," Kai protested. Gods, he needed some coffee and a shower. He felt like he had been stuck in some zero-g fight from hell and lost. It hurt to breathe, and he could feel himself bruising in places he didn't know existed. "We'd have to work. None of us know anything about freighters."

"We'll have to fake it," Brya said. She sounded like she was fighting not to collapse and weep. "We just have to get out of the Mibela System. The freighter will take us to Alliance space and we can start over there." She stamped her foot in frustration. "Damn it, Kai, *move!*"

Kai didn't think he could be more surprised at her news, but she'd managed to do it with the mention of Alliance space. "It'll take weeks to get to the Alliance on a freighter," he pointed out.

The wall that had knocked him out had a sizable dent where his head had hit it, and Kai thought he should probably see a doctor before they left. A pair of duffel bags was parked at the broken front door. Brya hadn't been kidding when she said she had them packed and ready to go. "I should go to an infirmary," he said.

"The ship has one. It's leaving in an hour. Dav's picking us up. *Move*, Kai."

"What'll happen if we stay?" he asked stubbornly.

Brya winced as she slung a duffel over her shoulder. Her answer was blunt, her tone flat. "They'll kill us. My mother will make sure we're dead, and your parents won't care at all. They're too embarrassed over something that's no one's business but mine. Ours," she added.

Kai would have expected to feel shock or anger at Brya's pronouncement, but instead felt nothing. An eerie calmness descended over him at his acceptance of her words. His parents truly didn't care what happened to him because of the way he was born. "All right. We'll go to the Alliance. What waits for us there?"

Brya looked outside furtively, waiting for Dav's wheeler to pull up. "I don't know," she admitted. "Dav thinks we should learn a few things on the freighter and join a crew when we get there."

Kai knew that "we" referred solely to her and Dav, and he would likely be on his own. Something in him twisted. "We're married. What about that?" he asked, voice quiet.

She looked at him like he'd lost his mind. Maybe he had from that knock against the wall courtesy of her mother. "Kai, come on. Our titles and the arranged marriage aren't recognized off-planet. We're not married in the Alliance, or in any other way, you know." She looked away.

Kai knew.

A dilapidated open-topped wheeler drove up beside the small house in the dawn sunlight, helmed by Brya's shifty-eyed boyfriend. He scraped his overgrown hair out of his eyes, revealing an ugly bruise across his forehead. Brya and Kai hurried out of the house and tossed their bags in the back of the vehicle. Brya climbed in the front seat beside Dav, and Kai in the back with the duffels. Dav grunted by way of greeting and gunned the engine, peeling down the cobblestoned street. "Took you long enough," he growled.

"Sorry, but Kai was knocked out."

"Huh," he said. "*I* didn't get knocked out when your mother stopped by."

Despite his headache, irritation flared through Kai. "Maybe she was tired by the time she got to your shithole," he snapped.

"Look, High Priest Tenth Seat or whatever the hell you are, if you don't shut up and show a little respect, I have no problem leaving you here."

"Dav," said Brya softly. She placed her hand on his arm. "Don't. He's my friend." She shot a glance at the back seat, one that told Kai to shut up.

He did, and the silence allowed him to panic about the new life waiting for him. He wouldn't even have time to bid farewell to his friends. "Do we have time to make a couple of stops? There are some people I'd like to say goodbye to."

Brya gave a short, bitter laugh. "Of course not."

"I just want to say goodbye to them and let them know I'm okay. That's all."

"No," said Dav bluntly. "Do you really think they'd care, anyway? Aren't your friends on the councils?"

"Not yet." The few that he had hadn't cared about his lack of telepathic talents, at least for the time being. Who knew how their friendships would have been affected when they eventually inherited their seats in government.

"I'm sure my mother already told the entire city about me and Dav," Brya said. "No one will want to see either of us."

Kai's eyes met hers, and she looked away, but not before she saw regret reflecting back at him.

The freighter was hot, cramped, and carrying illegal cargo. The surly captain hadn't said as much, but it was obvious based on the strict rules about not going near the cargo bays and how cagey the crew was whenever waystations or docks were mentioned.

Kai, Brya, and Dav were among a handful of Ralanians fleeing the Mibela System for the safety of the Alliance, the center of civilized space, and in the case of a few passengers, the Rims. Kai couldn't imagine why anyone would want to go to one of those planets. The living conditions could be cruder than on Ralani. The Alliance was their only real option, although he had no idea what he would do when he got there.

They crossed into Alliance territory after nearly five weeks drifting in space, during which they dodged pirate vessels and had a narrow run-in with a dwarf star when their ship's sensors went awry. There was always something wrong on this godsforsaken rust bucket, and Kai found the easiest way to pass the time and forget was to tool around with the ship's computers, all of which was new technology to him.

It wasn't just leaving the only home he'd ever known he tried to put behind him that rankled, it was also the impromptu marriage ceremony the freighter captain performed for Brya and Dav as soon as they crossed the border. Kai had smiled and stood politely aside as Brya legally married a scowling Dav, and then listened to her chatter about when their union would be filed and registered in the Alliance, when they finally reached a station. Brya had giggled like a little girl when the captain announced it and excitedly told Kai they were both free.

Their cargo was dropped off at an independent waystation on the border straddling Alliance and Rims space, and a few days later the remaining passengers were kicked off at Karys

Station with strict orders from the freighter's captain not to talk about their voyage. Kai had a pretty good idea what the freighter's crew could unleash on him if he disobeyed, and he never wanted to be beaten again. Weeks after leaving Ralani, he still had nightmares about Fika.

Dav and Brya scoured help wanted advertisements at Karys Station and contacted a small freighter company to join their crew. Kai considered doing the same on another ship, but couldn't see himself spending endless months in space aboard another clunky ship about to fall apart.

He had won some credits in a few card games while on board the freighter, and he booked a cheap room in the seedier sector of Karys Station to mull over his options, few as they were. He spent a few days wandering around the station's commercial sector, marveling over the noise and nonstop music and crush of people, and clusters of Alliance Fleet officers milling around pubs he couldn't afford to get drunk in. There was a military outpost on the station, and he downloaded some of their recruitment information to a datapad he found abandoned on a bench.

Military life beat a drab existence on a freighter. At the very least, the food was bound to be better.

Brya met with Kai at a dingy pub near his hotel the night before she and Dav were scheduled to leave on their freighter where they'd found work. Dav was gone, out at a pub with his new colleagues and getting falling-down drunk, as Brya laughingly described it. She and Kai drank tiny cups of overpriced beer and she asked if he had decided what he was going to do.

"The Fleet, I think," he replied dismally. He stared in his miniature beer glass. He had enough credits to stay one more night in his hotel and for a few more drinks. Then, he needed to find a more reliable source of income besides card games.

"Seriously? I never pegged you as the military type."

"What else can I do?" he asked. "I'm old enough to join."

"It's a twelve-year commitment!"

"Twelve years of guaranteed work."

"You could join the freighter crew with me and Dav," she suggested.

"No." Catching her raised eyebrow, he added, "Five weeks on that ship was enough for me. I'd rather be doing something for the greater good."

"'Greater good'? Gods, you've been reading too much of the Fleet's propaganda."

"I don't have a lot of other options." His voice came out sharper than he intended.

Brya immediately softened. "Yeah, of course. I'm sorry. For all of this. I really am." She looked at him, her deep violet eyes full of sympathy for the first time. She looked away. "I don't love her, you know. My mother. I never did. She hated that I wasn't a boy, and that I'm not a telepath."

"I know the feeling."

"I wish I'd stayed home that night," she confessed, surprising him.

So did Kai, but for other reasons. He would have stayed on Ralani if their relationship worked, or if she was even willing to try. *She couldn't,* he told himself. *She never knew you were willing, and now it's too late.*

He could tell her how he felt, but he didn't think that would solve any of their problems. It was likelier that she would get up and leave, and he would never hear from her again.

He changed the subject instead. "There's a Fleet ship docked here," he said. "The *Admiral Moore*. I spoke to a few of the officers today, and they said they can sign me up for the officers' academy. They leave in two days, and they can arrange to take me there."

"Why not just join up and start basic training right away?" she asked.

"I have more options if I go to the academy," he explained. "More training. I found out on the freighter that I'm pretty good with computers. I can do something with them if I enroll in the academy first."

Brya sighed. "If that's what you want."

It wasn't Kai's first choice, but it was the only viable one he had. "I do," he lied.

CHAPTER 2

Twelve years later

"We can do this the easy way or the hard way." The thug leaned in closer, his horrible breath puffing over Brya's face in a thick, odorous cloud. She forced herself to hide her disgust and keep a straight face.

"I don't see why you need me to do it," she protested. "I told you I'm straight. Me and my ship are legit. Find someone else."

"There's nobody else who knows the back star lanes or the Rims like you do, and nobody else who still owes Wethmore anything."

The mention of the captain of that godsforsaken freighter roused Brya's ire. "I don't owe him a fucking thing," she hissed. She tried to extricate herself from the man, whose hands were planted on either side of her head, holding her in place against the wall of the station's airlock corridor. Her small ship was docked just a few meters away. Maybe she could make a run for it.

She considered the man menacing over her. He was a full

head taller than she, and despite his unkempt appearance, he looked fit and strong. He could easily chase her down.

She hadn't seen Wethmore in nearly two years, not since her husband's death. She had left the bastard captain's employ and bought her own ship, the *Rapture*, and had been struggling to keep herself afloat ever since. It was hard being a brand-new, legit freighter operator just starting out, so much less profitable hauling spare parts across the galaxy instead of ungraded fuel or other things less savory. The *Rapture*'s necessary refueling at Karys Station had set her back a shitload of credits, and she was down to her last few between now and the next shipping job, whenever that may be.

"Wethmore might disagree," the thug said. Brya looked around the corridor, praying for someone to appear so he might run off and leave her alone. "He's still pissed that you bailed on that last job from the Rims."

Fear and indignation gave way to anger. "I needed to get away from him! I was finally able to buy myself out of that life. Of course I bailed!" And Dav had just died, although even if he had survived his accident, she would have left him anyway. But she didn't tell that to the thug.

He finally removed his hands from either side of her head and shrugged. "It's not like anyone's mourning Dav."

It was true, but she sidestepped the remark. "I'm sick of that life, okay? Tell Wethmore no, I'm not working for him." She held up her left hand, where the last two fingers had been severed. Her cheap metallic prosthetics shone under the station's lights. "See this? I've already paid for leaving Wethmore's operation. Fuck off." She ducked under one of his arms on either side of her head and started to walk away, but the man grabbed her and pinned her against the wall again. Brya refused to cow and forced herself to meet him eye to eye.

"He says he'll turn you in if you don't," the man said

smugly. "That'll be worse that losing a couple of fingers. He knows everything you've ever done, everything you've ever smuggled, every crime you've participated in and witnessed. You want to reconsider?" He released her arms but didn't back away.

Brya shuddered. How Wethmore had escaped being caught was so far beyond her, but justice could never be counted on in any part of space.

"He has everything you've ever done for him," the man continued. "Your name is on every manifest, he has your bio-code imprinted on every part of that ship. You'd be *fucked*, Dennir, and you know it. You couldn't even go back to your backwards home planet to hide."

He had her there. She couldn't go back to Ralani under any circumstances.

"What is it?" she demanded. "What would I be moving?" He opened his mouth to reply, but she held up a hand to silence him. "I'm not dealing with people, weapons, or drugs."

"Fuel," he replied simply. "Ungraded petrik. Just take it to a planet in the Outer Rims. We'll send you more instructions later. Your ship has a fortified cargo hold, so you shouldn't worry about explosions." He smirked at her. "Although after the way Dav died, you'd think you'd have those protections in place, anyway."

Brya itched to clock him one in the jaw on general principles, but that would only make things worse. "What do I get?" she demanded.

"You don't go to prison."

"I need money. I could be transporting spare parts for credits if I wasn't being blackmailed into this."

He gave her a look that questioned her intelligence. "Of course, you'll be compensated. Wethmore knows you're broke. If you do a good job like a proper little freighter captain, he'll transfer some to your ship's account as soon as it's loaded up with the petrik."

"And when will that be?"

"As soon as we leave the corridor," he said. "You spend another day at Karys Station, play like you're having a quick holiday from the demands of the shipping business, and then leave tomorrow. Your manifest will tell you everything else you need to know and we'll take care loading your ship."

Brya eyed him. "And this will be the last time Wethmore ever contacts me?"

"Promise. He doesn't like you very much, either."

Undoubtedly. Brya tried to school her expression to the one of hard-boiled freighter captain and nodded. "I'll do it."

Like she had a choice in the matter.

Kai didn't know what to do with himself. *Stupid furlough*, he thought. Then, *stupid me for getting shot in the first place*.

He had had enough medical care on his injured leg and wrist than he cared to remember, and they were still tender. He doubted his leg would ever be the same, because three laser hits meant he would always have a bit of a limp and it would act up in any humidity. But for now, he just wanted to be able to take a few steps without wincing in pain. It was embarrassing. His wrist was mostly healed and he would be returning to a desk job when his medical leave ended.

He would already be at his new desk job now, pending his reenlistment as his Fleet contract was nearly over, but his superiors had urged him to take a few weeks furlough to recover. Kai had refused, and the urging became an order. A lieutenant, no matter how talented he was with anything related to circuitry, couldn't be taking breaks every hour to change his skin regenerators and get local painkillers. It would only get worse unless he took some time off to heal.

Kai had argued every step of the way, but in the end, the Fleet won, and he packed a duffel and headed to Karys Station, the epicenter of Alliance space, for a few days. Back where his life started over, so many years ago.

He checked into a decent hotel when he arrived at Karys Station, a small room with a vidscreen, fully stocked replicator, and a water shower. The ship he was currently posted to, the *Starspot*, like all new ships, used a laser cleansing protocol instead of water in their bathrooms, and Kai wanted to treat himself. He briefly wondered if he would be allowed back on board the *Starspot* if he promised to stay in his quarters.

Kai finally resigned himself to having a few drinks in Mack's, a Fleet favorite. He picked a seat at the bar, only half-full at this early hour in the evening, and nursed a beer. Why was he feeling so withdrawn? Karys Station used to be one of his favorite spots, although it had always been a bittersweet place for him. It was where he got his start when he fled to the Alliance from Ralani, where literally whole new worlds had opened up and opportunity beckoned.

It was also where he had said goodbye to Brya.

Not a day had passed since then where he hadn't thought of her, even if it was only for a moment or two. He had met up with her twice by chance at different spaceports while he was in the academy, but other than that, he hadn't seen her in ten years. He had done some discreet poking around throughout the years and found that she had vague connections to a suspicious freighter captain, but nothing damning on her. Brya's trail had stopped cold about five years ago, as though she had dropped out of the galaxy, and that scared him a little. The lack of obituaries or news stories about her death had only marginally reassured him.

Still, he wondered how she was faring.

A minor commotion at the bar's entrance snapped him back to reality. A group of well-dressed women, one wearing a gaudy, spiky tiara whose fake gemstones spelled out BIRTHDAY GIRL, burst through the pub's doors, giggling, loudly talking about what they wanted to order, and just how much *fun* Fleet hotspots were. Kai willed them not to sit near him. It was an uncharacteristic wish. He usually had great luck with women at Mack's.

The gods told him no, and they took seats around him at the bar. He stared into his beer glass as they ordered drinks garnished with little crystals hooked on the rims.

"Hi," said one of them. She was tall, with a deep tan that indicated she wasn't someone stuck on a ship all day. Someone with money, or her parents' money.

"Hey," said Kai, and managed a small smile. *Go, please.*

"I've seen you here before," she said. "You're Fleet, right?"

He nodded.

"Where's the rest of your crew?"

"I'm on medical leave," Kai said.

That elicited melodramatic gasps from the other women. "What happened?" the birthday girl purred.

"It was an accident. I was hit with a laser rifle." Once upon a time, Kai would have used that to suggest playing Doctor.

"So you're a strong soldier, then," said the tanned woman. She leaned a little closer to him and he could smell her perfume over the scent of spilled beer.

Kai chanced a glance at her. She held her glass daintily in one hand, a sultry look on her face. She had to know exactly how insipid she sounded, but it must have worked for her in the past.

"Lieutenant," he finally replied. "I work in communications." There was no getting rid of them without being rude, so he leaned back in his seat and tried to summon the old Kai. "What do you ladies do?"

They tittered like he had just said something funny. "Stasia Bleek," the tanned woman said, like that name should ring a bell for Kai.

Her friends looked shocked at the lack of recognition. "She's the fashion designer," the birthday girl said. "I'm Nori, and there's Glad, Vivian, and Mia." She pointed at each person in their group, and Kai quickly forgot who was who.

"Lieutenant Kai Toric," he said. "Currently assigned to the *Starspot*."

"It doesn't stop by very often," commented Stasia, another inane remark.

Kai felt suffocated. He had to get out of here. This was not the night for picking up Fleet groupies. Not now or maybe ever again. "No, it doesn't," he said. "It doesn't have to refuel as often as the older ships." He drained his glass and stood up, pasting a wince of pain on his face. "I'm sorry, ladies," he said. "My leg is killing me. I have to head back to my hotel for the rest of the night." They cooed half-hearted protests, but he only smiled and shrugged. He laid a few credits on the bar, enough to cover the group for another round of drinks. "Have one more on me. I'm sure I'll see you later." They giggled, and he winked lasciviously. Stasia arched an eyebrow at him, and he knew immediately she didn't buy his story. "Happy birthday, Nori."

He remembered to walk out of the pub with an exaggerated limp. Once he was back in the commercial sector's carnival of lights and noise, he quickened his pace, heading to his hotel on the other side of the station and ten decks up. He leg twinged, and he looked for the closest moving sidewalk to take him across, but it was full with a lineup snaking behind it. He sighed and kept on, looking for another one.

Maybe it was a mistake trying to take a vacation on Karys

Station. It wasn't just being blindsided by a birthday party, since he'd already run into a former lover and a couple of one-night stands, one of whom had vowed to stick a knife in his ribs if he ever laid eyes on her again. The station itself had been looking different since he arrived on his own. For the first time, he was bothered by the constant noise and the bright lights. The vendors' overflowing stalls now appeared cheap and tawdry. If Kai didn't know any better, he would suspect the full-time residents of being robots programmed to be cheery and flirty to the point of being obnoxious. First thing tomorrow morning, Kai was booking a trip to one of the leisure worlds at the station's travel agency.

A commotion a few meters away held up the crush of people swarming along the commercial strip. Kai fought back a flare of irritation and picked his way around, seeing a pair of men, drunk by the sound of it, starting a fight. And people were shouting about bets. "For fuck's sake," he muttered under his breath.

Kai shook his head and tried to get out of the crowd, but it looked like he was stuck here for now. He heard a feminine voice calling, "Excuse me... I'm sorry, it's an emergency, thank you," and a slim form forced her way through the throng of people, smacking right into Kai.

"I'm sorry," she said.

"It happens," Kai replied, and glanced down at her. She held his gaze for a second, then her violet eyes blinked and widened.

"Kai?" she said hoarsely.

"*Brya*?"

Shock suffused her features. "Kai," she repeated. Quickly, she turned away and kept forcing herself through the people.

What the hell was she doing?

Kai followed her. If she noticed, she didn't make any sign of it, and he didn't want to alert her in case she took off running. Finally, they got through the knot of people, and in front of a perfume vendor he grabbed her arm and spun her around to face him. She shrieked, the sound swallowed by the roar of voices and thump of music. Her fear-glazed eyes fixed on his face, but Kai had seen that look before in combat. She was seeing something that wasn't there anymore.

"Brya!" he shouted over the noise.

She blinked and returned to the present. Her expression shifted to one of anger. "Let me go!" she snapped. "If you don't, then you're stuck with me." She wrenched her arm away. She looked around, but the only person who took any notice of them was the perfume vendor, who shouted something in one of the Alliance languages Kai didn't speak and shoved a fistful of samples at Brya. She waved him away.

"Stuck with you?" Kai said. "What do you mean? What kind of trouble are you in?"

"I'm not in trouble," Brya replied, and with shaking hands straightened her faded blue flight jacket. There was something odd about her fingers, and she caught Kai's curious look and shoved them in her pockets. She looked away. "It's nothing," she said.

Kai's minor empathic sense picked up fear, so palpable it vibrated. "Brya," he said gently. "If you're in trouble, I can help you."

She shook her head. "No, you can't," she replied. In the neon light offered in the darkened sector, he saw the exhaustion and stress in her face. Her lips were drawn in a tight line and there were shadows under her eyes. Her dark-blonde hair hung crookedly in curly tufts around her face and was streaked with faded colors, as though she had poured bottles of dye through it. She was thinner than she should be, exacerbated by the loose flight jacket and pants she wore. The pant cuffs pooled around her ankles, half obscuring her beat-up black boots. She was as far from ex-nobility as she could be and looked younger than the thirty years Kai knew she was.

Kai tried another tack. "At least let me get you a drink or something," he offered. "Or dinner. Are you hungry?" He tried to smile. "I was just thinking about you today, actually." And every day for the last decade.

Her gaze darted around the commercial strip as though she were looking for someone. "Okay," she relented. "A drink. Somewhere quiet."

CHAPTER 3

Kai led Brya through the station with a confidence she had never seen when they were newlywed teenagers. "Where are we going?" she asked nervously as they boarded a lift. She was afraid to run into one of Wethmore's henchmen, especially since she was in the company of a Fleet officer, if that was what Kai still did. He was wearing civilian clothes, dark gray pants and a black sweater. She couldn't see any sign of a weapon, doubling her anxiety.

"A quiet place near my hotel. It's a Fleet place," he replied.

Great. He was still with the Fleet. She didn't want to think about what Wethmore would do if he saw her hanging around an establishment that catered to the military, despite the fact that there was a good-sized installation on the lower decks. Wethmore didn't give a shit about that. He wouldn't only take her fingers if he found out.

They ended up in a nearly deserted hole in the wall on the ninth deck, where Brya had never ventured on her trips to Karys Station. It was far out of her league: too upscale, too clean, too expensive. She kept her head down and avoided looking at the uniformed military milling around this sector and didn't raise it until she and Kai took seats at the back of the restaurant.

"What do you want?" he asked. The question was amiable, but she heard the authority in his voice. His demeanor matched the dominating figure he made now. He wasn't the skinny kid with fashionably overgrown hair he had been on Ralani. He had grown up, and in another lifetime, Brya would have found him attractive. Hell, she did already, but this wasn't the time. She willed herself not to notice that.

"Just a beer, please."

"Are you sure?" he asked.

"Yes, I'm sure that I definitely need something alcoholic right now," she said peevishly.

"I mean, do you want something to eat?" He eyed her across the table, taking in the clothes that ballooned around her. She *was* hungry. The replicator on her ship had died a few weeks ago and she had been living off freeze-dried rations and whatever she could pick up on stations and spaceports since then.

"Yes," she replied, chastised.

He gestured to the menu pad on the table. "Get whatever you want," he said. She looked at the prices and blanched. "It's my treat," he added, eyebrow raised at her reaction.

She tabbed in an order for stew, deliberately using her right hand and keeping the left with its cheap metal prosthetic fingers under the table. She couldn't help but smile a little in anticipation. It would be her first hot meal in a long time. Kai ordered his own food and thoughtfully regarded her across the small table.

"So," he said. "Am I stuck with you? I'm on medical leave, so I have the time."

She remembered her panicked words on the concourse and felt like an idiot. "I don't know why I said that," she mumbled.

"What have you been up to all this time?" he asked.

She fumbled for words. "Working on freighters. I have my own now, the *Rapture*. She's nothing fancy, but I like being my own boss. I guess you're still with the Fleet?"

He nodded. "Lieutenant in communications, but I'm switching to a desk job and I can focus on coding and development. I'm working on a new transport unit code that won't make people so sick." A server stopped at their table with their drinks, a real person and not a bot.

When she glided away, Brya whispered, "Where's the food?"

He chuckled. "Hungry?"

"Well, yeah, but why wouldn't she bring it with her?"

"It isn't replicated here," Kai explained. "It's cooked from scratch."

That explained the prices. Brya doubted she'd had a home-cooked meal since she left Ralani. "Oh," she said, feeling even more foolish. "Do you cook?"

"No."

An awkward silence fell over the table. Brya looked at their surroundings, taking in the soft lighting and quiet atmosphere, and feeling like a grubby kid. Kai finally leaned forward and said, "Tell me what's going on. I can help you."

She shook her head. "It's nothing, really. Just an old colleague who's pissed off. I'm not a threat to his business, but he's still pestering me."

"What about Dav?" Kai asked. "Where is he?"

Her answer was clipped and came out more brusque than she intended. "He died two years ago. It was an accident with unstable cargo."

Kai's eyes widened in surprise. "I'm so sorry," he said genuinely.

"Don't be." She took a deep breath. "It wasn't going well the last few years of our marriage, and his stupidity killed him in the end." She held up her hands in frustration. "That makes me a horrible person to say that, but it's true. You don't just walk into a cargo bay when a fuel container explodes."

Kai nodded and spied her left hand.

Shit.

He grabbed it in a firm grip that she couldn't wrench away from, zeroing in on the prosthetics, fitted above the knuckles where her fingers had been cleanly sheared off. "What the *fuck*?" he said in a hoarse whisper. "How did this happen? Who did this to you?"

She yanked her hand free. "It was an accident," she lied. "A console caught fire on an old tanker I was working on, and..."

"That wasn't an accident," he argued in an angry whisper. "I've seen accidents before. The rest of you doesn't look like it's been in an electrical fire. You don't lose just two fingers in one, either. Your entire hand would have been *charred*. Why didn't you see a doctor? The bone and tissues could have been regenerated."

She stared at him icily. "Okay, you got me. It wasn't an accident. But I'd prefer not to talk about it."

The server reappeared at their table, dishes in hand. Kai and Brya murmured their thanks and she dug into hers, momentarily forgetting their argument. Gods, she hadn't eaten like this in years. She had to force herself to not to start shoving everything on the table in her mouth as fast as she could.

"Just answer one question," Kai said. "Then I'll drop it."

She reluctantly set down a piece of still-warm bread. "Okay," she said cautiously. "But I don't have to answer it."

He took a deep breath. "Did Dav do that to you?"

She almost laughed at the question. *Dav*? Her late husband had been an idiot and blindly followed whatever orders Wethmore issued, but he hadn't been a sadist. "No."

She returned to her meal, and they ate in silence until the dishes were clean.

"Do you want dessert?" Kai finally asked.

Oh, hell, she could eat half a dozen desserts. "Yes, please."

"Good. They have a cart here. We'll get a little of everything."

Brya was comfortably full when they left the restaurant, for the first time in what felt like forever. She and Kai stopped at his hotel, a small, cozy building a deck above. "Thank you," she said awkwardly. "I guess this is where we go our separate ways." *Again*, a voice added in her head. "Do you have a datapad? I could give you my ship's transmit address and we could keep in touch this time."

Kai dug through his pants pockets and produced his handheld, presenting it to her. She thumbed in the *Rapture*'s address and handed it back. She didn't want him to know she was too scared to return to her ship right now. It was probably being loaded with the ungraded fuel Wethmore had blackmailed her into hauling. She didn't want to be anywhere near it until she was ready to leave, in case one of the station authorities found it and arrested her. She didn't have enough to spare on a room. She planned to spend the night in one of the seamier cafés below the commercial strip that served bottomless coffee for half a credit.

As if he could read her mind, he asked, "Where are you going?" For all she knew, maybe he'd had latent telepathic abilities manifest since their flight from Ralani.

"I have a room booked on deck three," she lied, then mentally kicked herself for it. Deck three was kitty-corner to the barracks the Fleet used when a ship docked at Karys Station.

He stared at her, and she looked away. "Okay," he said finally. She met his gaze again. "It was good seeing you, Brya. I wondered, you know." He paused, searching for words. "If you ever need any help, contact me. No questions asked."

She nodded and wished she could. "Thank you."

They shared an awkward hug, and he let himself into the hotel. She turned down the corridor to go to the lower decks.

And immediately saw a familiar face in profile. Wethmore's hired thug.

She froze on the spot, unsure what to do. He didn't turn his head, but when he did, he would see her, and she wasn't sure she could talk herself out of this situation. She had never told Wethmore that she had been married before she married Dav, even if it wasn't recognized off her home world. It wouldn't be hard for someone like him to find out more about Kai and do something to him. She couldn't let that happen.

She turned away and fled into the hotel.

CHAPTER 4

Kai's hand was in his room's palm lock when Brya called his name and jogged toward him. His eyes widened in surprise. "I need help," she said before he could say anything.

He nodded, clearly unsurprised to hear that. He pressed his hand into the lock, releasing the door. The room's lights cycled on automatically, highlighting the spare, windowless space. There was a wide bed taking up most of the room, a replicator, a desk and vidscreen, and a small bathroom off to the side. Kai shut the door behind them and faced her.

"You need to tell me what's going on," he said. He pointed to the chair locked to the desk. "Sit."

She obeyed and glanced around the room. Like the restaurant, it was far nicer than anything she could afford. "Um, why aren't you staying in one of the Fleet's places?" she asked, stalling. Nervousness twisted in her gut. Maybe dragging Kai into this was a mistake. "You must be getting gouged here."

"I'm not letting you change the subject, but since you asked, I was supposed to take a regular holiday and a hotel is part of that. And yes, I'm getting gouged, which is why I hope

no one from the front desk saw you. They'll double my bill."
He crossed his arms over his chest. "Tell me."

"I don't think anyone saw me."

"*Brya*."

The warning in his voice was unmistakable. Who could blame him? She had run away with another man and dropped off his radar for a decade. He had already been more generous to her than she deserved, and if she stayed, she was going to drag him into her own shitstorm. She had no right to heap this on him. She'd made yet another mistake. "I'll go," she volunteered, and stood up.

His hands pressed down her shoulders until she was planted back in the chair. A frisson of awareness jolted through her but she pushed it away. "Okay," she said. He sat down on the edge of the bed and leaned forward, elbows on his knees.

A sigh escaped her lips, and she was in danger of crying for the first time in years. She hadn't even cried when Dav got himself killed, only when Wethmore took her fingers. But there were concessions that had to be made first. "If I tell you, I need you to keep the Fleet out of this," she said. Kai aside, she would always harbor at least a little fear of the military and law enforcement.

"That depends on what you're into."

"I need you to do this for me." She didn't bother trying to hide the pleading note in her voice. "A lot of it is my fault, but I've been doing things right for the last year. Or trying to." She would *not* cry, would not let Kai think she was trying to manipulate him. That was something the old Brya would have done and what he was probably expecting. She closed her eyes until the tears receded, then began her story.

"You remember when we left Ralani?" she said, and he gave her the barest of nods. Of course, he would remember their escape. "We arrived here, and you signed up with the military and Dav and I joined a freighter crew. We worked that ship for a few months before we heard about a better-paying operation with Angel Transport. Have you heard of them?"

"I've heard of them, but I don't follow the transport business."

"Dav and I took jobs with them for about a year, and he met a guy who was starting his own business, Pace Wethmore. He's from one of the planets in the Outer Rims, or that's what he said. I didn't like him, but I didn't know why exactly." She paused. Wethmore had been polite and respectful to her in the beginning. At the time, she hadn't been able to put her finger on it why she disliked him. There was something off about the man, like an evil aura surrounding him she couldn't actually see. "He and the stuff he was talking about seemed too good to be true," she continued. "Dav fell for it, and I didn't know what else to do, and I loved him and wanted to be with him. I ruined all of our lives for him, after all. So I joined Wethmore's crew."

"And it turned out to be too good to be true?" Kai guessed. He sidestepped her comment about her ruining their lives. He already knew that.

"Yeah," she said. "I'm sure you know most small-time operators move something shady from time to time to stay on top of things, and no matter what the Fleet thinks, most of it's harmless. Almost everyone moves untaxed liquor at least once. It pays pretty well, and if you get caught, you're only stuck with a fine. No one dies or gets hurt. I was expecting an occasional booze run with Wethmore, but I found out fast that *nothing* he was doing was legal. It was the worst kind of shit to be hauling across space, too. Ungraded fuel, drugs, and sometimes people." She shuddered and had to fight back tears again.

"Why didn't you go to the Fleet or transportation authorities?" Kai asked.

"Wethmore knew people," Brya said miserably. "I don't know if that's true or not. I've been in Alliance space for twelve years and I'm *still* not sure how things work that way. But he told everyone on his ship that if anyone blabbed, he'd find a way to track us down and kill us."

"What did Dav think of all this?"

"Dav didn't care," Brya replied. "He and Wethmore were friends, and Dav was like his disciple. Before we met him, we'd been talking about using the money we'd saved up to buy a ship of our own and run our own freighter business, but once he met Wethmore, that was it. He was never leaving him, and that meant I wouldn't either. Dav never hit me, but if Wethmore told him to, he would have. He was so devoted to Wethmore that he walked into a firetrap and died." She looked at the carpet. "Gods, he was an idiot. We both were."

"So Wethmore was running a smuggling operation, then," Kai said.

"Yeah, he smuggled everything illegal you could think of."

"And you escaped." Like all of his contributions to the conversation, Kai kept things short and to the point. He was definitely Brya's idea of a military man.

"Sort of. I bought my way out," she explained.

Kai raised an eyebrow, but otherwise kept his face impassive.

"I'd tried to escape before, and I had the shit beaten out of me," she confessed. "Twice before Dav died. I tried hiding out at spaceports but Wethmore or one of the crew always found me. Dav didn't do anything about it, and he couldn't see why I wanted to leave. He was being paid well and Wethmore liked him. When Dav died, Wethmore and I had a talk and he said I could go under a few conditions." She looked down at her left hand and its metal prosthetics. "I had to give him most of Dav's money. I kept enough to buy a ticket to Prime and find work on a freighter there, but everything else went to Wethmore." She faltered. "Ten days before we reached the spaceport where I would catch a flight to Prime, he cut off my fingers as a warning."

As she spoke the words, she remembered the searing pain of Wethmore's laser scalpel, the smells of burning flesh and bone cooking under its heat. The sight of her bloody fingers, their polished nails winking in the lights overhead, on the floor. Two years later, she still had nightmares about that night.

"I went to Prime with my hand bandaged," she said, forcing herself to continue. "I went back to work at Angel Transport and lived in employee housing to save money for my first year on my own. Angel was bought out by Renascent Galactic Transport six months ago, and I bought the *Rapture* around that time instead of signing on with them. Now I'm moving perfectly legal cargo. Spare parts, EVA suits, that kind of thing. I won't even move a single bottle of untaxed whiskey.

"Everything was going fine until today. Someone who works for Wethmore found me here after I docked for refueling, and blackmailed me into moving ungraded petrik to somewhere in the Rims. He threatened me and after he let me go, I ran into you in the commercial sector. That crowd was dumb luck. A few drunks were kicked out of a bar and started a brawl. Did you see it?"

"I only saw the crowd, not the fight. And you agreed to this delivery?" Kai's voice was flat and his eyes expressionless.

"It was either agree to take the fuel or Wethmore would have killed me. I saw the guy who forced me into it again in the corridor outside your hotel, and I came in here. I don't know if he saw me or not." Her voice rose. "I don't want to be tortured or killed or mind-wiped. I don't want to go to a prison colony, and we both know that's where smugglers end up. I'm sure you know what the consequences are for accomplices. Being a stupid person who tries to keep a marriage together at any cost doesn't make me less of an accomplice. Feeling like shit about what you're doing doesn't make things magically better." She stood up and began to pace the small room.

"Why don't you go to the Fleet now?" Kai asked.

"And tell them what?" she said. "I'd probably be going to a prison colony for twenty years."

"You were forced into that life. You were abused."

"I'd still be completely fucked, Kai. Wethmore would find a way to track me down and do away with me and make it look like an accident. He's done it before." She stopped her pacing. "I'm just going to deliver the fuel and try to disappear. It's easier that way."

"What if I could help you?" he asked.

"How?" She squashed the flare of hope that burned as soon as he made the offer, not letting herself be disappointed.

"I tell the Fleet what's going on," he said. "You deliver the fuel, but we trap Wethmore. Would that work?"

The hope returned, bright as ever. "You could do that?" she said. "What are you in the Fleet, anyway? I thought you were a lieutenant."

"I am. I'm not that high up," he said. "But I know people who could help you. You must know how the Fleet feels about human smuggling and drug trafficking and murder. You can help us catch them."

"And what would happen to me?" she asked.

"I don't know. I can find out."

The tears that had been threatening spilled over and she started to cry. She was mortified, but couldn't help it. "Why?" she said between sobs.

"Because Wethmore's a piece of shit," he said simply. "And

because both of us left Ralani to start over and you deserve to start over like I did." His expression softened, and he opened his arms. "Come here."

Obediently, she let him hold her, the feeling of him settling and reassuring. She couldn't remember the last time she felt safe like this. His breath ruffled her hair, stirring a feeling inside her she couldn't identify.

"Now, where are you going for the night?" he asked. "Tell me the truth."

She pulled away reluctantly. "I'm not going back to my ship until I have to," she confessed. "It's supposed to leave with the fuel at fifteen hundred hours tomorrow."

"So, do you have a room anywhere?"

"No. I was going to a café on the lower decks to drink coffee and watch a serial all night."

"Stay here," he said. "I have weapons if someone breaks in. I'm not at top form at the moment, but I can still shoot."

Brya realized that in all of her wallowing, she hadn't asked why Kai was at Karys Station. Once again, she felt selfish and ashamed at her self-centeredness. "What happened?" she asked.

"There was an accident on the ship I'm assigned to. Some idiot ensign with more brawn than brains was showing off in a training exercise I was leading and shot me in the leg and wrist."

She gasped.

"It's fine. I work in communications, but I do a lot more than just that." He straightened. Pride tinged his voice with his next words. "I redesigned the way comm badges work and made them more efficient. They can now be used in a greater range, including outside the ship they're programmed to. That's very useful in emergencies and rescue missions."

Brya was unsure what to say to that. "Congratulations."

He smiled, and her stomach flipped a little. He changed the subject. "Look, we can't risk Wethmore's hired thugs finding you. Don't go to that café. Which side of the bed do you want?"

He couldn't be serious. She shook her head. "I'll sleep on the floor."

"Just pick a side, Brya." He dug through his duffel and produced an oversized t-shirt. "You can sleep in this." He handed it to her.

"Um."

"I'm helping you, Brya. Obviously, Karys Station isn't the best place for you to be right now. We'll get up early tomorrow morning so I can notify the Fleet of the situation and get this sting set up." He gestured to the bathroom. "You should wash up first. It's a water bathroom."

Brya's boat had a water shower, but it worked only intermittently. She stepped into the bathroom and was delighted to see it had a full-size tub. She was about to ask him if she could take a bath, but held back the request. He was probably paying for water consumption and the last thing she wanted to do was take even more from him.

As if he could read her mind, he said, "Take a bath. For what they're charging me, the water's included."

The small pleasure ahead of her brought a smile to her face, the first in a long time. She looked at him over her shoulder. "Thank you."

She closed the door and left Kai's shirt and a towel on the small vanity and ran a bath. While the water was running, she finger-combed her hair and made a face at her reflection in the mirror. She looked like she hadn't slept in days, and she hadn't, not really. The night before she docked the *Rapture* at Karys a bunch of kids goofing off in their parents' shuttles on the Landen star lane had roused from sleep at three hundred hours. She had no idea how they managed to find that back route, and they had set off her intruder alarms and fueled her panic. Little bastards.

The tub full, she turned away from the mirror and stripped off her clothes. She climbed into the hot water —*heavenly*—and tried to turn off her brain for a few minutes.

———

Kai didn't want to go to the Fleet base on station in case Brya's pursuers had followed her. Instead, he sent a transmit and notified his commanding officer on the *Starspot* of a possible major smuggling operation.

Captain Setroff and Commander Darby stared at him through the transmit vidscreen. Kai braced himself for an onslaught, and he received it.

"You're supposed to be on medical leave!" Setroff roared.

"I am," Kai said. "But wouldn't you be doing the same thing if you ran into *your* ex-wife who you separated from on good terms?" Of course, he knew now that wasn't the case for Brya.

"Couldn't say. I've never had one," Setroff replied..

"She needs help, and I believe her story about this Wethmore. We have a chance to nail this guy. He abused her and lets his crew members die due to his negligence."

"Why didn't she go to the Fleet before?" Darby asked.

Kai explained Brya's reasoning, her ignorance of the law in Alliance space. Darby nodded. "Good points," he agreed. "The Fleet could file charges, but if she has evidence like you say she does, she would receive immunity. Has she told anyone else about this?"

Kai shook his head. "Not a soul until I ran into her on the commercial strip."

"Good. The Fleet will take care of it, and if she's telling the truth, she won't go to a prison colony or undergo a mind wipe. But if she's lying about anything..." Darby glowered at Kai through the monitor.

"She isn't. You know me and you know what I can pick up. She's terrified, and she isn't lying."

"You sure you're not an empath, Lieutenant Toric?" Setroff said.

It wasn't the first time he'd been asked that, no matter how many times he'd answered in the negative. He tried not to let his irritation show when he replied. "I'm not an empath. You know that. I just read body language well." That wasn't entirely true, but he didn't have anyone to ask about empathic talents emerging in adulthood.

"Okay, we'll help you with this. Send her out to wherever this petrik's supposed to go, and we'll ambush whoever is on the receiving end," Setroff said. "We'll notify the Fleet and the *Starspot* will get the assignment. Are you sure her ship can handle that kind of cargo?"

Kai nodded. "The *Rapture*'s holds are fortified. Her husband died in an explosion in a cargo bay a couple of years ago, and I think she's pretty paranoid. I'll still check her ship's specs before we depart Karys Station."

Kai told him what little he knew of the flight plan, with a promise to keep in touch. "We'll send her our transmit address on the untraceable links," Setroff promised.

"No need," Kai said. "I'll tell her myself. I'm going with her."

Setroff and Darby were silent for a moment. "You're still on leave!" Setroff repeated.

"You already yelled at me for being on medical leave."

"Watch it, Lieutenant. You're still my subordinate. And I yelled at you for getting involved in this without notifying the Fleet base on station."

"Captain, I told Brya I would stick with her until this is over, and I intend to."

Realization dawned over Darby's features. "Well, Kai, you do have a reputation to keep up," he said.

Apparently, both of them had forgotten that their commanding officer was present, because Kai shot back, "Fuck off, Keith," he snapped, using the commander's first name. "I'm not that much of an asshole. I wouldn't try anything with her." Though in another lifetime, maybe... "She's in trouble."

"Language, both of you!" Setroff shouted. "You're on a military channel. You are not Captain Bartha, you're not in a bar, and this is not shore leave. Show some fucking respect." The captain realized what he had just said, and his lips thinned. Despite the situation, Kai felt a bubble of laughter well up in him, and when he glanced at Darby through the vidscreen, he saw the commander was fighting the same thing.

"Permission to speak freely, Captain?" Kai said.

"Granted. Provisionally," Setroff added.

"With Captain Bartha's retirement, the Fleet needs another hard-assed, foul-mouthed captain. I think you fit the bill."

He and Darby erupted into gales of laughter. Setroff glared at both. "Zayna Bartha was one of the finest officers I had the pleasure of serving with, so I'll take that as a compliment," he said. "She knew what she was doing."

"Setroff threatened to show an admiral the airlock from the outside when he tried to reprogram the comm badge channel to factory specs," Darby revealed. "Couple of days ago."

"Sir, you are the new Bartha, sir," Kai said. "And thank you for keeping my program in place."

Setroff muttered something in his first language, one that was spoken in Alliance territory closer to the Rims. Finally, he said, "Okay, Lieutenant, permission to accompany Miss... whatever her last name is on this mission."

"Dennir," said a voice from the bathroom. She had opened the door, letting humid air escape, and she was finger-combing her damp hair in the mirror.

"Brya Dennir," Kai repeated to the vidscreen. She'd kept her original name, then.

"You'll depart tomorrow as scheduled, and both of you will get in touch with the Fleet over the military channels," Setroff commanded. Kai nodded, and they signed off.

"They didn't want to talk to me?" Brya said.

Kai turned to face her. His shirt hung nearly to her knees, and she had slipped back into the pants she was wearing earlier. She had found the room's provided toiletries and was now brushing her teeth. She caught his glance and said, "What?" around a mouthful of toothpaste.

He took her being nearly dressed a cue that he would likely have to sleep close to fully dressed, but shucked his sweater, revealing his t-shirt. "Nothing."

"I like this place," Brya said. She set the toothbrush next to the sink. "My ship is half lasers and half water. Do you ever get stuck using cleansing protocols on your teeth?"

"No, the military isn't that cheap. They're only in the showers." He turned on the vidscreen by the bed and scrolled through the broadcasts. Brya hovered near the replicator and flicked through the menu screen with her fingertips.

"It feels a lot cleaner when you're using water. Do you want anything?" she asked, gesturing at the replicator. She ordered a cup of tea.

It so reminiscent of their brief life together, the comfortable friendship that once made him imagine could develop into something more. Except they had always maintained separate bedrooms. "No thanks." She sat down on the bed, carefully holding her teacup. "Tell me about your boat," he said.

"The *Rapture*? She's a used F-class freighter. She has her

problems, but she's built solid and the cargo holds are reinforced like I told you," Brya said. "I liked her because she has three holds and her previous owner modded it so one person can pilot. Eventually all the consoles and wiring will have to be replaced, but I'm not thinking about that right now." She smiled wistfully.

"What about weapons?"

"A non-functional laser cannon that I can't afford to have charged. But it's not like hauling spare parts across Alliance space is particularly dangerous." She sighed and drained her tea. "The water distribution sucks, like I said before. The guy I bought her from installed that cleansing protocol I told you about, and that makes up for it. But the replicator is fucked and I haven't been able to fix it, and the hyperspace engine makes grinding noises when I hit a gate. Or it did the last time I went through hyperspace. That sound scared me and I haven't since. Intership communication works about eighty percent of the time. I occasionally have trouble uploading flight plans."

A hyperspace engine was easily fixed if one had the money, which she clearly didn't. A laser cannon could be charged for the same reason. He could repair the replicator and possibly the water system without any trouble.

She sank back into her pillow, a blissful expression on her face. Concern spread through him at the sight of it. "Please tell me you have a captain's cabin on the *Rapture* and you're not sleeping on the cockpit's deck," Kai said.

She turned over on her side and glared up at him. "Of course I have somewhere to sleep. I'm just enjoying not worrying for my life for a few hours. Did you find any good vids?"

"A couple of films and a few news broadcasts. That's it."

"One of the films, then."

"One's targeted toward the, um, lonely gentleman. Is the horror one okay?"

Brya laughed. Kai felt some of his own tension radiating from him, and something else. A rightness and familiarity he hadn't experienced since leaving Ralani. He didn't know until then how much he had missed her.

CHAPTER 5

Brya didn't want to wake up, and she squeezed her eyes together to fight off the encroaching light. She pulled the blanket over her head and snuggled deeper into the bed. That was better. An arm snaked around her side and pulled her more tightly against him, and she sighed, content. She felt something hard press against her backside, warm breath against her hair, and her eyes flew open before she turned around in bed to face a still-slumbering Kai.

Mortification swept over her in a wave. "Oh, gods," she muttered.

He woke up at her movement, his arm still carelessly splayed across her hip. His eyes widened. "Good morning," he said, and quickly withdrew his hand.

"Morning." She pulled away sat up in bed. She kept her eyes focused on the replicator across the room as the lights slowly cycled on, hoping he couldn't see the furious blush she knew had to be spreading across her face.

"I'm sorry," he said. "That was an accident."

She nodded. "I figured."

"That... happens in the mornings," he explained.

"Yeah, I know."

Brya fought the urge to giggle, knowing Kai probably wouldn't appreciate it. Dav hadn't, not in all the years they had been together. "What time did you set the alarm?" she asked. "The lights are already coming on."

He checked the clock inset in the wall. "Another half hour. My original plan was to get up early and book a trip at a travel kiosk before all the best destinations were reserved."

Brya relaxed and settled back in the covers. "So it's not imperative that we're up at five hundred hours?"

"No."

"Good." She drew the blanket back over her and steered the conversation back to their situation. "Any idea of when the Fleet will be getting in touch?"

"Not until later in the morning, and we're not contacting them on your ship until we're out of communication range with Karys Station."

"So I can sleep for another hour?" They'd gone to bed early by her standards, but she hadn't slept so well in months. Embarrassment aside, waking up with Kai's arm wrapped around her protectively had been a nice surprise, although she couldn't admit that to him.

"If you want to." He reset the alarm and ordered the lights off, and Brya nestled back into her warm cocoon of blankets. Kai moved to the other side of the bed, giving her space.

Sleep eluded her, and she could tell by his breathing that he was still awake, too. "Kai?" she whispered.

"Yeah?"

"How safe is all this? I'm used to being chased and everything, but it's never been officially sanctioned by the Fleet."

"Why are you whispering?"

She sighed and sat up again. "I don't know."

He rolled over. In the dim nighttime lights, she saw him

make a face. "We'll both be fine, I think. I wouldn't have volunteered in my condition otherwise."

"Will doing this make things worse? The *Rapture* doesn't have an infirmary, just basic first aid equipment, and it's a few years out of date." A few decades was more like it. Her boat was forty years old.

"No. I have some regenerators and pain patches with me, but the worst is over. Anyway, there won't be a lot for us to do between here and when the Fleet steps in. I can fix your replicator and take a look at your water system." She heard the smile in his voice and wondered how bored he'd been since he took medical leave that he'd be excited to do that for her.

She'd already taken enough from him. She shook her head vehemently. "No," she protested. "I won't allow it. You've already done so much for me and I don't want to take advantage of you anymore."

"You're not taking advantage. I offered to help you, and I'm offering to fix your replicator. I have something to lose if it doesn't work, too. I like eating regular meals and showering in hot water. The Fleet spoils me that way."

Brya remained tight-lipped about that. She felt guilty enough for imposing herself when he was supposed to be recovering from laser strikes without letting him tinker with her ship.

"Besides, I eat a lot. Do you have enough food on there for two people?" he asked.

He had her there. "Shit," she muttered.

She got out of bed and padded through the darkened room to the replicator. "I don't think I'm going back to sleep. Do you want anything?"

"There's a big breakfast option on there," he said. "I want that." He ordered the lights on and got out of bed, stretching. The muscles in his arms and back flexed under his t-shirt and she couldn't help but stare for a moment, breakfast temporarily forgotten. He caught her looking and smiled. She felt herself flush and turned back to the replicator to tab in their orders.

He turned on the vidscreen, picking up a Karys news broadcast, and they ate in bed. "We used to do this on Ralani," Brya recalled before she could stop herself.

"Yeah, in the master bedroom. The vidscreen there had the best reception." Vidscreens and galactic broadcasts were looked down upon on their home planet, but had been slowly gaining acceptance by the time they left. He eyed the two full breakfast platters on the bed. "Are you sure you can eat that much?"

"Definitely." Brya helped herself to a plate of eggs. "I can't believe this is from a replicator. It tastes like the real thing."

They cleaned their plates and were on their second cups of coffee when the computer chimed an incoming transmit. Kai glanced at the screen. "It's the Fleet." They both stood up and straightened their clothes before he thumbed the "accept" tab. Brya hovered in the background as Kai spoke with someone in a Fleet uniform loaded with insignia before she was commanded to speak.

He introduced himself as Admiral Falta, and listed off a stream of credentials and areas of responsibility that Brya promptly forgot. Finally, he said, "Please tell us of your association with this Captain Wethmore. Everything we've looked at indicates that he's a law-abiding freighter operator."

"It's easy to make people think that when most of your deliveries are to the Rims," she said. "It isn't that difficult to fly under the Fleet's radar when you're rarely in the Alliance's inner worlds. It's totally different there and worse in the Outer Rims."

Admiral Falta stared at her stonily through the screen. "I'm not trying to insult the Fleet," Brya said. "It's just that it's easy to not get caught, especially when your operation is so big."

"Why should we believe you?" His voice was cold.

"I get that you don't have any reason to. I'm willing to cooperate in any way the Fleet wants, and I promise I'm telling you the truth."

"You were willing to cooperate with Wethmore," the admiral pointed out.

Anger flashed through Brya. She held up her left hand. Her metal prosthetics flashed silver at the vidscreen. "He cut off my fingers when I stopped," she snapped. "And I'd appreciate if you looked at this from my point of view." From behind the desk, Kai shook his head, but she soldiered on. "I arrived in Alliance space twelve years ago from the Mibela System, from Ralani. Do you know how things work over there?"

"I have a working knowledge of that part of space, yes." She could tell Falta was fighting to keep his temper in check, but she didn't care. She wasn't one of his minions, and she knew she had precious little to lose. Except her freedom, a voice reminded her in the back of her mind, but she tamped that thought down. She was *not* going to let this admiral push her around.

"Well, it's ass-backwards," she replied. "It's like living in a bubble. Most people never leave. Kai—Lieutenant Toric—and I were forced into marriage when we were seventeen and kicked off the planet when we were eighteen. Neither of us had any idea how to live when we left. Joining a freighter crew seemed like a good idea to me, and I found out the hard way that it's more isolating than living on Ralani." She paused, trying to keep herself from derailing her train of thought. "To be honest, Admiral, these two years on my own were the first where I've truly been in charge of my own life, and I'm learning a lot, also the hard way. I've never dealt with the Fleet.

I don't have a clue how. So, yeah, I cooperated with Wethmore, because I didn't have a choice. I saw what he can do when he's pissed off." Falta opened his mouth to speak, but she cut him off. "I can tell you everything I know. I have names and copies of manifests and transmits in the *Rapture*'s databanks." Assuming Wethmore's hired thug hadn't taken a look around her computers and delete those hidden files, but she didn't tell the admiral that.

As she said the words, she realized another reason she hadn't turned to help until now: no one would have listened to a nobody freighter captain. Whenever she saw news reports about the Fleet, they had always served the interests of *important* victims. The rich investors bilked out of their savings, the missing heiresses living it up on leisure worlds without telling their handlers, the expensive private star yachts stolen from governors' homes: these were the crimes investigated by Alliance law enforcement. No one really cared about the underclass in the Alliance, or if one smuggler killed another.

She and Falta glared at each other through the screen, waiting for the other to speak. Finally, Falta cleared his throat and in a restrained voice said, "All right. We will investigate your claims and you have the Fleet's cooperation. One of our patrol ships will be at the rendezvous point where you are to unload your cargo, and Lieutenant Toric will be keeping in touch with the Fleet during your journey. However..." He leaned forward. "If at any point we discover you are lying to us, or keeping any information from us, you will not receive any amnesty from the Fleet. Is that understood?"

"I expected that," Brya said. "I'm not a total idiot."

Kai cringed.

Falta glowered at her for another moment, and Brya stared right back at him. "I would like to speak with Lieutenant Toric," he said icily.

"Of course," she replied with exaggerated politeness, and stood up. She walked to the bathroom without another word.

Kai immediately took the seat at the desk. "Admiral," he said crisply.

"We expect regular communication with you via military channels and your remembering that you're supposed to be on medical leave. You'll to be in touch with Interior Security and your commanding officer on the *Starspot*. It will be the patrol ship assigned to that area, and it is equipped to handle a mass arrest."

Having been assigned to the *Starspot* for the last three years, Kai already knew that, but he nodded anyway. He and Falta exchanged a few more forced pleasantries before signing off.

He leaned back in the chair and pinched the bridge of his nose. "That was Admiral Falta," he said.

"What's your point?" Brya called from the bathroom over the sound of water flowing into the tub. She returned to the bedroom, defiance written across her features.

"He can be difficult and a know-it-all, but he's still the commanding officer for a quarter of the Fleet. He's in charge of all the patrol ships and battleships. He's not someone you want to piss off."

"I know what I'm doing on a freighter," Brya said. "I know I'm new at living like a normal person, but I can pilot a ship blindfolded and I know more about the civilian star lanes than the Fleet does, I guarantee it." She turned to the wall-mounted mirror and made a face, picking at her hair. "I really need my comb," she muttered.

"When did you do that to your feet?"

The abrupt change of topic and the curiosity in his voice caught her attention. She looked down at her bare feet, at the elaborate tattoos of stars that extended from their tops up her legs, hidden by her oversized trousers. The work was done in glittery black and silver laser ink. "A few years ago."

"Where else did you get inked?"

He sounded intrigued, but there was something else in his voice, a note she'd never heard from him before that made her stomach flutter. It was a thoroughly inappropriate reaction considering the circumstances, and she tamped it down. Her reply was brisk. "A few other places that are decently hidden right now. Do you have a datapad, and does it have anything interesting on it?" She hoped he didn't notice the breathiness in her reply. She wasn't used to feeling off-kilter because of him.

"Yes to both. Why?" he asked suspiciously.

She went to the replicator and ordered a cup of tea. "I wanted to read or watch something in the tub. I'm taking advantage of it for as long as I can."

Kai found his datapad in a side pocket of his duffel. "I have a few files on here that'll fit the bill. Nothing too heavy or sad."

Brya tabbed it on and scrolled through the serials and vids saved on it. She settled on a popular serial and opened the file. "This will do nicely." She picked up the teacup from the replicator and stepped into the bathroom, closing the door behind her with her hip.

She settled into the tub, the tea balanced on its side. The first episode of the serial was projected against the bathroom wall, a silly thing with melodramatic acting and budget special effects, not the kind of thing she would expect Kai to enjoy. She couldn't focus on it thanks to the man who was on the other side of the door.

If this were another time and place, and if she and Kai hadn't been forced into an arranged marriage, if she hadn't deserted him, if she wasn't dependent on him to live, she would be giving serious thought to going back in the bedroom naked and seeing what happened from there.

The idea gave her pause. She held a handful of soap powder in her hand, not noticing as the grains slid down her arm to foam in the water as she ran over the scenario in her mind. She'd never considered Kai in a romantic or sexual light until this morning.

Their banter aside, the same things they had joked about when they were married, there was no indication on his part that he was remotely attracted to her, and besides, he was Fleet now. Besides all of that, she had been truly awful to him.

She let herself wonder how her life would have turned out had she stayed with Kai when they fled Ralani as she sank back into the water, ignoring the serial playing out on the wall. She knew now that it would have been the right thing to do, even if they hadn't stayed together as a married couple. She'd had a bad feeling about her marriage to Dav within a few months, and by their second anniversary she had stayed with him solely because she had nowhere else to go. He and Wethmore had made sure of that. Brya would have gladly gone to the Fleet if she thought she had a chance of surviving beyond a few weeks away from the merciless smuggler.

She quickly washed her hair and felt some regret when she drained the water. She wouldn't be getting a bath again any time soon. She dressed in yesterday's clothes and returned to the hotel room, Kai's dry datapad in hand. She presented it to him dramatically. "You have eclectic taste in entertainment."

"Well, I try to be a man of culture." He nodded and went to the bathroom to take a shower. "I'll be out in a few minutes, and then we'll talk about our strategy when we leave."

Brya was a nervous wreck when she finally went to the civilian docks. She and Kai had agreed it was best that they not be seen together once they left their room, so she had slipped out of the hotel via their side entrance an hour before he checked out. The Fleet outpost had conveniently arranged to have a small passenger shuttle docked next to the *Rapture*, which Kai would pretend was his, should anyone be watching the area. When he was inside, someone hiding on board the shuttle would pretend to be Kai and depart the station, and Kai would be transported to the *Rapture* via the shuttle's unit when they hit the safety of space.

She checked in without incident and paid the docking and refueling fees with the near-last of her credits. "Have a good time on station?" the dockhand asked.

She nodded. "Always."

"Your friends loaded cargo on your ship per your instructions," he said. "You know that isn't regulation here, but they had your authorization."

She nodded again and kept her hands tightly clenched in front of her to keep them from trembling.

He fished around in a battered metal desk and came up with a datakey. "The first one asked me to give this to you. Fenton, I think he said his name was."

She nodded and kept the fear out of her voice. "I was expecting this," she said. "Thank you." But something the dockhand said stopped her from leaving right away. "The *first* one?"

"Yeah, two guys dropped by, about two hours apart. I only got Fenton's name."

"Oh. Well, thanks." That was weird, but so was this whole situation.

She quickly made her way to the access corridor and let herself into the *Rapture*'s dock, shivering in the cold. No matter how well-maintained docks were, it was impossible to keep the areas regularly exposed to space warm. A few other ships were docked nearby, locked into the station, but she didn't see another soul. The ship's door opened and its ramp extended with her palm print and retinal scan, and she walked up it gratefully. Despite her troubles, the *Rapture* was her home. The boat wasn't pretty or especially fast, but it was hers.

She ran a diagnostic when she powered it up, finding nothing suspicious in its results. She checked her starboard cargo bay and saw it was loaded with the ungraded fuel, and the bay itself was fully operational. Its doors were sealed and locked down in the event of combustion. The malfunction or outright lack of lockout doors on freighters were the reasons accidents still occurred in space.

A voice broke through the comm system. "*Rapture*, retract your ramp and seal the doors. Dock two has requested permission to depart." Right on schedule, the Fleet's shuttle was leaving the station. Brya pulled up the ramp and closed the doors in preparation. Through the starboard viewport, she saw the access corridor's safety lights change from green to yellow as the dock's sensors checked for life forms. A warning alarm blared through the docks, and the lights changed to red as the airlock next door released the shuttle.

"We may as well kill two birds with one stone," Brya said into the comm. "My flight plan's uploaded. Did you get it?" Her flight plan was bogus, listing a route that was supposed to take her to a tiny moon orbiting Pentalon. She'd change it after she read her instructions from Wethmore. Freighter operators did that all the time.

"Just popped up on my screen."

"*Rapture* requesting clearance to depart."

"Cleared for departure. You're free to go, Captain."

Brya keyed in her command codes to launch the ship from the dock. It smoothly unlocked itself from the station, and from the aft monitor she saw the airlocks cycle shut. "See you later, Captain Dennir," said the dockhand.

She said goodbye and put some distance between her and the shuttle before hailing it. "Kai?" she said.

"Right here. Sikra has the transport unit ready to go, just say the word."

"You have my exact coordinates?" Brya disliked transporters. Every damn time she had gone through one she had left her lunch on the floor.

She could hear him roll his eyes across space, and she grinned. "Of course. I'll be on your bridge in a minute."

"Bridge?" she repeated and looked around the cockpit. It was too small to be called a bridge, and could barely fit both of them.

He materialized behind her, his duffel in hand and a greenish cast to his face. "The Fleet hasn't approved testing for my new transport code," he said.

"Why not?"

"If something goes wrong, you could turn into molecular soup. I haven't had a lot of volunteers." He looked around for somewhere to sit and sank into the unused copilot's seat.

He leaned over, touching his forehead to his knees. "That was rough," he said. "Smaller units are always bad." He gingerly lifted his head and looked around the cockpit. "So this is the *Rapture*?"

"Just the cockpit," she said. "The cargo holds, engine, and control rooms are belowdeck, and the living area is through the back." She pointed to a door on the opposite side of the tucked-in ramp and set the ship to autopilot. She produced the datakey Fenton had left for her from her pocket. "This was left for me when I checked out of the docks. It's supposed to have instructions on it." She found a compatible port on a computer built into the wall. Kai grabbed her wrist before she could plug it in.

"It could be a trap," he said. "It could trigger an explosion or launch a tracker."

"Kai, that's stuff you learn your first month in smuggling," she said, exasperated. "That's why this computer exists. It works separately from my primaries and can't infect any files."

"How often do you get stuck with these kinds of assignments, anyway?" he asked suspiciously.

"This is the first time since I went legit. The previous owner had this installed. I usually use it to play music or vids when I'm working." She fitted the datakey into the port.

The contents were exactly as Fenton had described them: written instructions to take her cargo to a small planet in the Outer Rims, a round-trip journey that would take the *Rapture* at five to seven days given that her hyperspace engines were currently useless.

"Ishka," Kai read on the screen. "I'm not familiar with that planet. You?"

"I've heard the name, but I've never been there." She saw Kai eyeing the pilot's seat. "I told you not to get any ideas. This is *my* ship." She keyed in the amended flight plan. At least Ishka wasn't too far away from Pentalon. The switch wouldn't raise any red flags.

"I can help."

"Have you ever worked in navigation?" she asked. He shook his head. "How about a freighter?"

"No, aside from the one we took to the Alliance."

"It's a lot different than flying one of your fancy Fleet ships," she said. "Autopilot is actually useful on these ones." She crossed back to the controls, where she looked up the best way to chart a course to the unknown planet. Her estimate of how long it would take her boat to get to Ishka was correct. They were looking at a minimum five-day journey, not including a stop for refueling on the way back. Kai followed her and peered over her shoulder as she examined the star charts saved in the computer.

"Impressive," he said. "I haven't seen these routes before. How many people actually use them?"

"Anyone who has a commercial transport ship knows about them," she replied. "They're not secret. They're just not used as often because there aren't a lot of hypergates in them and communications get spotty in some areas. The Landen star lane is one of my favorites to use when I go to the Rims." She tabbed through the star charts displayed on the computer screen and plotted a course using the Landen lane. If she used that route, she wouldn't have to be at the controls for a few hours, at least until the lane turned into an asteroid field, which would require manual piloting. The asteroids were spaced far enough apart so it wasn't completely treacherous. She he never worried too much about it.

"Let me show you the rest of the ship," she offered. Kai nodded and followed, duffel in hand.

The area off the bridge was a modest living space. There was a combination galley and lounge, equipped with the malfunctioning replicator and laundry machine. Off that area was a pair of small bedrooms separated by a bathroom. Like all the doors on board, they weren't automatic, the previous owner having replaced them for reasons unknown. She slid open the door to the spare room and gestured for Kai to step inside.

"It's nice," he said appreciatively. "I mean that." He dropped his duffel on the floor and sat on the bed, massaging his leg.

"Are you okay?" she asked.

He nodded. "The transporter didn't help. That's part of what I'm trying to fix with my new project." He stood up. "Lead on."

The stairwell to the lower deck was accessible through a

doorway beside the laundry machine. There she showed him the engine room and her pitiful first aid station. "Don't get sick," she said. "I can only afford to keep this at the minimum requirements. The dispensary has enough medication to treat a bad case of food poisoning or a severed finger, but that's it. It would have been useful when it happened to me." She didn't bother to hide the bitterness in her voice.

"Just out of curiosity, why weren't your fingers regenerated?" he asked.

Without thinking, she curled her hand into her palm, doing her best to hide her prosthetic digits. "I couldn't get to a clinic in time," she said. "You have three days tops to start bone regeneration. When I stopped screaming, Wethmore treated my hand just enough so I wouldn't get an infection, and it was another week before I was dropped off at Prime. It was too late."

"Brya," he began, but she cut him off.

"It's okay," she said. "I've adapted. I'm just grateful he didn't cut off a hand or foot or outright kill me. He was certainly capable of it, but he liked Dav enough not to." She held up her left hand and inspected it, the metal shining under the cockpit's lights. "I'm used to it." She arched an eyebrow at him. "Does it put you off?"

"No," he said, and strangely, she believed him.

She pointed to the various panels in the room. "There's life support, gravity, shields, and weapons. Everything important works."

"Except water and the replicator."

"I have enough water to live, and not having a replicator won't make me die in space," she explained.

"Can I take a look at them?" he asked.

She bit her lip. She really didn't want him doing any more for her.

"Come on," he wheedled. "I don't like being bored, bad things happen. Busy hands are happy hands."

"They teach you that in the Fleet?"

"Not in as many words, but yeah."

"Okay." She saw his point. "I'll give you the passwords to my primaries, and you can see what you can do."

CHAPTER 6

The drumbeat of pain had Kai awake at seven hundred hours the following morning. His leg and wrist throbbed. He hobbled out of bed and dug a couple of pain patches from his duffel and cursed the transport unit on the Fleet shuttle as he stuck them to his leg. After a moment, the aches subsided enough for him to limp out of his bedroom and take a quick shower. The stall's showerhead spit out a few drops of water before it groaned and switched into the backup laser mode. As he dressed, he thought about ways to fix it.

Brya was already wide awake in the cockpit, expertly guiding the *Rapture* through an asteroid field. The asteroids were small, but close enough together that the ship would need someone at navigation. Music blared from the computer where she had read the instructions, something loud and angry that wouldn't have been out of place in the kind of clubs Kai used to frequent. "Good morning," she said without turning her head. "We'll be out of here in about fifteen minutes, and then I'll see what I can dig up for breakfast. There are some coffee cubes and a kettle in the galley, if you want some."

So, she hadn't tried out the replicator yet. He had tweaked

it enough last night to produce a few basic dishes that tasted decent and were far more nutritious than the stuff in packets she had in her galley. He wanted to surprise her. "I'll wait for you."

He sat down in the unused copilot's seat and stole a glance at her. Her hair was pinned back with a couple of sparkly combs, and she wore black pants and a jacket over a purple tank top that fit better than the clothes she'd been wearing at Karys Station. "I didn't hear any alarms," he said, shifting his glance to the asteroid field beyond. "When did you get up?"

"I had the autopilot set to stop the ship twenty minutes out from the asteroid field," she said. "I set my alarm for when I thought we'd hit it, and I was right." An asteroid drifted dead ahead of them, and she cleanly steered around it.

"You don't get worried about asteroids?"

She shook her head. "Not the ones I have to deal with. The star lanes freighters use exist because they're safe." She patted the navigation console like it was a beloved pet. "I know what my boat can handle."

He watched as the asteroids became smaller and more spaced apart until they disappeared. He stole glances at her and was heartened to see the fear that had glazed her eyes yesterday had disappeared, revealing a serene and confident pilot. He took in the curve of her cheek as a small smile played across her lips at the sight of the starfield beyond, the way her eyes lit up.

She was happy.

Her fingers danced over a few controls as she turned the ship back over to autopilot. She stood up. "Let's see what I can dig up for breakfast."

"Let's see what your *replicator* can dig up," Kai said as he followed her. "I fixed it."

She turned around, astonished. Kai halted and nearly stumbled into her. "Already?" she asked.

Any reply he would have voiced evaporated. His breath caught in his throat. She was standing about a hand's width away from him, her mouth turned up in surprise. He caught the faint scent of perfume, something delicate, citrusy, and familiar, the same scent she had used when they were kids. And then he was a weak-kneed teenager again, awestruck in her presence and too intimidated to do anything about it. He wished he could lean forward and kiss her, something he had wanted to do since he saw her again at Karys Station.

Concern replaced the delight on her face. "Kai?" she said. "Are you okay?"

He mentally shook himself. "Yeah."

In the galley, Kai demonstrated the mostly restored replicator. "The whole unit will need to be replaced in the next couple of years," he said. "You probably already knew that. But it can make a few meals now, and better than the stuff you were eating before."

Brya tapped at the cracked menu screen and read the selections. They weren't nearly as vast as something a new replicator could offer, but she didn't seem to care. "You should pick the first meal. What do you want?" she asked.

He keyed in a request for eggs and toast, and she followed suit. She set the plates at the small table locked to the deck and ordered some coffee.

The look on her face was blissful as she tasted her breakfast, and he couldn't help but smile at her reaction. "Perfect," she breathed. "Thank you. How did you get that fixed?"

He shrugged. "I had some codes in my datapad saved for just this occasion. I used to tweak the replicator in my cabin on the first ship I was posted to so I could order food I actually liked. I played around with your hardware a little, too. The big problem was a damaged sensor, and I replaced that."

"You keep spare sensors in your luggage?"

"You never know when they'll come in handy." He took a swallow of coffee. "I'm going to take a look at your water system, too." He held up a hand when she opened her mouth to argue. "It's not just you I'm doing this for. I don't like laser cleansers. And if I'm busy doing that kind of thing, I won't have time to be a backseat pilot." Or stare at her like an infatuated teenager, but he didn't mention that. It wasn't like he could act on that, anyway. Even in his younger and stupider days he wouldn't have dreamed of starting something with someone under his protection, or as vulnerable as Brya was right now.

Still, he was going to do his best to repair faulty water lines in space if it meant seeing that look of delight on her face again.

Brya had taken the longest shower she ever had since she bought the *Rapture* when Kai gave up tinkering with the ship's hardware that evening. She had relished the entire six minutes of hot water, and dismissed Kai's apologies for not having it fully functional. The taps at the sink worked, and it was much easier to brush her teeth with water than one of the laser wands built into the ship.

She and Kai shared a dinner of meat stew in the evening: hot, fragrant, and tasting far better than something reconstituted from a packet. She had checked the ship's progress along the Landen lane before she went to bed, and guessed they would have about six hours before she needed to be back at the controls.

Brya had hoped to fall into a quiet, dreamless sleep, something that had eluded her for years. She felt fairly safe now that she was back in the serene familiarity of deep space, and because she had another person on board. No, not just another person. *Kai* made her feel safe.

Being Ralanian without telepathic or empathic talents meant she wasn't subjected to visions or other peoples' dreams and nightmares, a trait that now made her grateful to be a regular person. Her nightmares were strictly her own: violent re-imaginings of her life with Dav and Wethmore, of abuse, fear, and outright war in space on unarmed vessels. She *did* know when she was sleeping during a dream, and from her years in the Alliance knew that wasn't normal among other humanoids. They had decreased in frequency since she moved aboard the *Rapture*, but not intensity.

Her wish for a peaceful sleep wasn't granted. Now she was back on Wethmore's freighter, loaded with a questionable weapons array and an outright illegal shield that hid their identification from Fleet patrol ships. She tried to force the dream away, hoping to will herself into remembering playing with Kai when they were little, before they were forced into their betrothal. It didn't work.

She smelled the smoke that had permeated throughout the ship after the fire that killed Dav, still hanging thickly in the ship's air. Another crew member had been bitching about docking at a station to let it air out properly, and Wethmore had yelled at him to shut up, they couldn't dock until they had delivered the remains of the second shipment in the other starboard cargo bay, and the rest of the ship hadn't taken much structural damage. Brya had spent the two days after the accident in a state of shock and worry, terrified that the vessel keeping them alive in the vacuum of space would fall apart. She was always nauseated from the smell, and there was nowhere on board that it hadn't leached. It was a mix of burned fuel, metal, and beneath that, the horrifying stench of roasted flesh. She hadn't protested when Wethmore opened up the cargo bay doors and let everything inside be sucked into space, not caring that Dav hadn't received a proper interment. She didn't know if a spineless, mean-spirited pirate like her husband deserved that dignity, anyway.

And you do? She had been sickened and ashamed at that thought. No, she didn't either.

The scene unfolded like it had so many nights over the last two years.

"I want to leave when we get to the next spaceport," she told Wethmore.

His nose wrinkled into distaste beneath his shaggy, unkempt mop of black hair, like he had just noticed that his ship smelled like death. His dark eyes narrowed. "Where the hell would you go?" he said.

"I don't know," she said. "But I can't do this anymore. You do your thing, I do mine."

Wethmore had regarded her thoughtfully for a moment, and the ball of dread that had formed in Brya's stomach moved to her throat. "I won't say anything," she said, her voice stuttering over the words, and forced a laugh. "Who would believe me? I just—I want my own life now."

He moved a step closer to her, and involuntarily she stepped back. She tried another tactic. "I'm useless to you without Dav. He's the reason you've kept me around so long. I can't lift heavy things, I can't fix the computers."

"You're a good pilot," he pointed out. "You're an excellent navigator."

She didn't know how to answer that. "Thank you, I guess."

Wethmore threw his hands up. "Okay, Brya. You win. We'll be docking at Crystal Station in twelve days, and you can leave then."

She couldn't believe she had bought her freedom so easily. "Really?"

"Really. But I have a couple of conditions," he said.

The nausea returned, full force. "What are they?"

"I want everything of Dav's. I'll leave you enough for a ticket to wherever you need to go, but I gave him everything. I didn't give it to you. I want it back."

Brya almost laughed out of relief. She had been expecting something much worse. "Of course," she said.

She should have known that wasn't the end of it.

Wethmore wrenched her out of bed in the middle of the night a few days before they made the station. "What the hell?" she said sleepily as the cabin lights sputtered, then cycled on. She tried to pull her arm out of his grip, but he wouldn't let go.

"Get up," he said, his voice a growl. "Get your ass in the lounge." She reached for a sweater to throw over her pajamas, but he shoved her forward. "Go!"

Heart pounding, she padded in bare feet to the lounge. A few crew members milled around, drinking coffee from the replicator and quietly complaining at having to get up in the middle of the night. They straightened when Wethmore stalked into the room and pointed to the long communal table in the centre. "Sit." His voice brooked no argument.

Brya obliged and took her usual seat near the end. Wethmore sat across from her.

"What's going on?" she asked. "What have I done now?"

"You know damn well. You didn't think I'd just let you waltz off this ship, did you?"

"No," she said, feeling like an idiot. She should have known Wethmore wouldn't just let her go. "But you're taking everything of mine and Dav's. What more is there?"

"Not much more, I promise," Wethmore said. "After this, I won't have to bother you again, and you'll know never to fuck with someone like me."

"I already know that," Brya told him, keeping her voice even. What was he planning?

"Give me your hands," he said. A few of the crew exchanged glances, like they knew what was coming.

"Why?"

"Just do it, or this'll be a lot worse."

Tentatively, she laid both hands on the low tabletop. His calloused fingers picked up each and examined them, like she was showing off some fine gems to sell and he thought they were fakes.

"Captain, what are you doing?"

He let her left hand drop to the table, and stood up. "Stay still." He turned to the navigator. "Hold it." The navigator obliged, and he pressed a meaty paw onto her wrist, pinning her hand to the table.

"What are you doing?" She couldn't keep the panic out of her voice.

Wethmore produced a laser scalpel from the pocket of his flight pants, and she screamed. "Don't! Not my hands! I told you I wouldn't say anything!"

"Relax, I'm not taking your hands," Wethmore said, boredom creeping into his voice. Brya tried to pull away from the navigator's grip. His hand pressed harder into hers, and she shrieked again. "But if you don't keep quiet, I might."

The scalpel's laser hovered over her hand, and Brya cried out at its heat above her hand. Wethmore deliberated over her fingers before cleanly slicing off the last two.

Her body thrashed in pain, and the navigator let her go. She tumbled to the floor clutching her hand, and it didn't register for a few seconds that the inhuman screams bouncing off the lounge walls were her own. Blood seeped through her fingers and spilled to the floor.

She saw Wethmore's boots on the decking, and he swept something off the table. *Her fingers!* She screamed again, tears pouring down her face. The captain wrenched her to her feet, but she didn't let go of her hand.

"Gods, they weren't even the whole fingers. Fucking hell, I don't know why Dav put up with you." He held out an antibiotic patch and slapped it on the back of her uninjured hand. "Don't take that off, you don't want to get an infection."

"Why?" The word came out in a strangled sob. Her throat felt raw from screaming.

He forced her back into her seat, and she felt sticky wetness seep through her pajamas. There was blood everywhere. How could a couple of fingers produce so much?

He didn't answer her question. "Give me your hand."

"No!"

"Do you *want* an infection?" he said. He wrenched her hands apart and held out a cauterizing laser. The fucker wasn't even going to use an anaesthetic.

The sear of the laser against her wounds brought another scream to her throat, then everything went black.

She woke up as she always did from this dream, crying and thrashing in her sheets. But this time she couldn't move, and she thought wildly that Wethmore had found her and was on board her ship. She screamed again, and she was let go, falling back on the pillows.

"Brya," said a soft voice.

She opened her eyes and tried to focus in the dim light of her cabin. Kai crouched beside her bed. She sat up and scrubbed at her wet eyes.

"Are you okay?" he asked.

"Yeah. It was just a bad dream. I'm fine." She sucked in a deep lungful of air, grateful to be alive. She curled her hand into a loose fist, the feeling of her metal prosthetics against her flesh and bone fingers always a stark contrast against her palm.

He settled on the edge of the bed. "You're sure?"

Why did she even try lying to him? He would always see through her. "They happen sometimes," she confessed. "I'm sorry I woke you up. I should've warned you I scream through nightmares sometimes."

"It wasn't just that," he said. His expression darkened. "I felt it."

Her eyes widened as she took in the implication. "You saw it," she said flatly.

"No," he corrected. "I *felt* your panic, and I woke up."

"Like a telepath."

"No, then I think I would have seen what was causing your distress. I told you I can sense extreme emotions. It started about a year after I signed up with the Fleet. I may be a very half-assed empath, but I'm not sure."

"Does that happen to Ralanians?" She didn't want to talk about her nightmare, and Kai seemed to pick up on that.

He shrugged in the darkness. "I don't know. I don't have anyone to ask about that. Sometimes I think that the stress of leaving Ralani triggered it."

"If we had known, maybe you wouldn't have had to lose your inheritance and leave."

"I would've lost my inheritance anyway," he said. "You have to a complete telepath to take a seat on the council. Empaths are just as looked down upon as we were."

"It's my fault you had to leave Ralani at all," she said softly and looked away. She fisted her hands in the bedsheets.

His next words were careful, as though he didn't want to offend her. Brya didn't see why he was being considerate when she didn't deserve it. "Everything that happened," he began, and paused. "I don't know why. Things haven't turned out like either of us planned."

"I deserved everything I got for what I did to you," she said in a rush. He stiffened. "I should've grown up and not kept up my relationship with Dav. It's *my* fault everything went to hell. *I'm* the reason we had to leave. And now I'm in trouble, and you've shown up and helped me and repaired things on my ship and you shouldn't have, not after what I've done."

He paused, carefully parsing out his words. "I wasn't mad about Dav," he said.

"You should have been! We were married!"

"We were *kids*," he said. "And I wanted you to be happy. I knew what we were getting into. It was an arranged marriage, Brya. No one's ever happy or even faithful in those things on Ralani. We were both embarrassments to our family, and it was the easiest way to keep us out of sight. Things worked out for us better than most arranged couples. I didn't want my personal feelings to get in the way of that."

"Personal feelings?"

He started a little. Brya thumbed on the light switch beside her bed to the lowest setting. The illumination panels set near the floor flickered on. She breathed in sharply when she saw he was shirtless, the dim light playing over lean muscles. There was a fading scar on his wrist from the accident on his ship. She was temporarily struck dumb at the sight, but she regained her voice. "What feelings?" she repeated.

He had a look on his face like he had just been tricked into selling Fleet secrets to the enemy. "It was nothing," he said.

"Tell me," she said, then added, "Please." She was almost afraid to hear where he was going with this.

He raked a hand through his sleep-disheveled hair. "I liked you, is all," he said.

Her heart skipped a couple of beats. "You *what*?"

"I liked you. That *way*, as the kids say. More than that, I thought." He locked gazes with her. "I was hoping it would turn into something more, but it didn't. I never told you, because I knew you didn't feel the same way, and you were happy with Dav. I thought if I said anything, you'd move out and we wouldn't be friends anymore. I wouldn't have had you in my life."

A fresh surge of guilt washed over Brya, and she groped for words. "I wish you'd told me."

"What for? Would it have made a difference?"

"I don't know. All I can tell you is that you don't know how sorry I am and how much I would change if I could."

"Me, too." He stared down at his hands. "And I'm sorry I got so pissed off. I shouldn't have, not when you had that kind of nightmare. What was it about?"

She held up her left hand. "When Wethmore did this."

"Do you want to talk about it?"

She shook her head. "It was just a replay of what happened that night. I don't get them as often as I used to, but when I do…" She looked away and sighed. "They're bad. At least I haven't dreamed about Dav since I bought the *Rapture*. I used to have that one a lot, when the cargo bay blew up." She paused, not wanting to discuss the accident. She pushed aside the blankets and got out of bed. "I think I'll get some juice. Do you want some?"

"Sure." He followed her to the galley, where she produced a bottle of juice and a pair of glasses from the small refrigerator beside the replicator. They leaned against the counter in comfortable silence.

Brya drained her glass and set it in the dish recycler. "Thank you again for all of this."

"You're welcome," he said. "Do you feel a little better?"

"Yeah."

He put his glass in the recycler and held out his arms. "Come here."

Brya let him enfold her in a hug, surprised at how much she needed it. She wrapped her arms around his neck and his slid behind her back. He was warm and solid, and underneath the scents of soap and sleep she could smell *him*. Her senses heightened, and she had to fight herself to keep from tasting the bare skin of his shoulder. His body stiffened perceptibly.

She wondered for a panicked moment if he could sense what she was thinking. No, she told herself. He said he could only pick up strong emotions, and she wasn't salivating over him. Yet.

His head dipped and he whispered in her ear, "Do you think you'll get back to sleep?"

His mouth next to her sent a happy buzz through her, and she couldn't help but shiver a little. "Yes," she murmured into his neck.

Kai's arms tightened around her, and his lips grazed the skin below her ear. Brya inhaled sharply, every nerve in her body prickling. For a second she thought he must have made a mistake, but he gently kissed the side of her neck again, and a small mewl sounded in the back of her throat. She moved her head and he lifted his, and nose-to-nose, they wordlessly caught each other's eyes.

This time his mouth covered hers, in an innocent, almost chaste kiss. Brya gently kissed him back, sweetly as if he had just brought her home after an evening at a cinema, but inside she was trembling. An excited awareness flooded through her body, something she hadn't experienced with anyone else and didn't realize she could feel until now. She couldn't help herself from kissing him again and immediately he deepened it, flicking his tongue against her willing mouth. She parted her lips and he responded with a groan, his tongue sweeping against hers possessively. Kai lifted her on to the galley counter and she was faintly aware of the salt and pepper shakers falling over. He took her face in his hands and he kissed her again, and she hooked her legs around his back. Breaking the kiss, he drifted his hands down her neck, her shoulders, to delicately trace the outline of her breasts through her thin pajama top, teasing her nipples. She arched her back at the light touch and reached for the hem of her shirt, but he grabbed her wrists as soon as her fingers touched the fabric.

"Brya, this is a really bad idea," he said softly. "I shouldn't have done that."

"We're both adults," she said, and tried to pull him back to her, but he stepped away.

It took a moment for her lust-addled brain to process what he was saying. She reluctantly disentangled her legs when she saw he was serious, and her body screamed at her when she realized he was probably right. "Damn," she finally said. She slid off the counter, her bare feet slapping against the deck's tiles.

"We should go back to bed," he said after a moment of awkward silence.

"Yeah." She was mortified. She shouldn't have tried to take things further. Certainly Kai had made the first move, but he had been sweet and downright *romantic*, and then she had to go and spoil it by essentially offering to let him have sex with her on the counter. Gods, he must think she was willing to do that in exchange for his help. Her face grew hot, and she was in danger of crying again. And her body, traitorous heathen it was, was still mourning his taking his hands off her.

They faced each other at her bedroom door, embarrassed, and in Kai's case, still aroused as she could see through the fabric of his loose pajama pants. She felt a savage triumph at knowing she wouldn't be the only one going to bed frustrated. "Good night, Kai," she said.

"Good night."

She closed the door behind her, and fell into bed, knowing it would be difficult to get back to sleep.

CHAPTER 7

Kai and Brya didn't speak much in the morning beyond perfunctory greetings. She busied herself with studying star charts in the cockpit, and he holed up in his room and tried to read a Fleet-issued engineering text on his datapad. By early afternoon he had re-read the same module and still couldn't absorb any of the information inside. Irritated, he set it aside.

He couldn't stop thinking about what had happened only hours before. Over and over his mind replayed the sensation of her lips against his, the feel of her body, the citrus scent of her hair. It was maddening. Twelve years ago he would have leaped at the opportunity to take what she was offering. Now, he had some scruples. If he had done what his body had urged him to do, he would have violated one of his few firm morals. She was in danger. He was supposed to be her protector.

"Kai?" He heard her call his name from the cockpit. He got off the bed.

Something resembling music drifted out of the wall-mounted computer, a slow electronic beat that made him grateful he couldn't hear it from his room. She was tapping around on the command consoles in front of her, periodically checking the deep space beyond. A yacht passed by. "Is something wrong?" He slid into the co-pilot's seat.

She shook her head. "Not yet. There's a minor fuel line break. It's happened before." His stomach turned over. Panic must have registered on his features, because she smiled and said, "Don't worry about it. There's a spaceport about two hours away from here where I can fix it. I'm on good terms with the staff there, and they'll rent a dock to me on credit."

She was being way too calm about this for his comfort. "You don't worry about spontaneous fuel line breaks in space?"

"There are safeguards in place," Brya replied. "Life support will still run and the ship will still move. We just have to get our asses to that spaceport." Her hands grazed the controls as she changed course. "It'll take a couple of hours when we get there. I know exactly where the break is and before you say anything, you're not helping. You've done enough, and you're still on medical leave. Besides, I don't want anyone there to see you."

"Do your friends at this spaceport know Wethmore?"

"I don't know, and I don't want to find out. I started docking and refueling there after I bought the *Rapture*."

He nodded. He was relieved to feel the tension from their early morning indiscretion fizzling out.

"Kai," she said quietly.

The tension returned. He knew what was coming.

"About... what happened," she said. She turned to face him. He turned his head. If he swiveled his seat around their knees would touch. He wanted to cut her off, apologize and ask her to forget it, but words failed him.

She grasped for them, too. "I... it was awkward," she said finally.

"Yeah." *Awkward* didn't quite cover what he'd had to sleep with last night.

"Just so you know," she said, and forced a small laugh. "Wow. I've never had this kind of conversation before. Um…" She self-consciously tucked a hank of blue-streaked hair behind her ear. "I know it looks really bad, but I wasn't trying to, well… offer payment for what you've done for me." Her cheeks flushed scarlet.

Kai felt his own face grow hot. "I wasn't trying to collect." Despite their mutual mortification, he felt relieved by her admission. "I don't know what got into me," he said. "I'm sorry about that."

"You don't need to apologize," she quickly assured him. She hesitated. "It was…" She stumbled over her words. "It was nice."

Nice? *Nice?* Kai struggled not to take offense.

Her eyes searched his face. "Say something," she said.

"I don't usually hear *nice* to describe my techniques."

"Well, what kind of words *do* you hear?"

Shit. She had him stuck there. "I don't usually take up with wordsmiths," he said.

She laughed, genuinely this time. "Well, I'm not a *wordsmith*," she said, exaggerating the last word. "But just because I'm not singing your praises in four languages doesn't mean…" She trailed off.

His pulse quickened. "What?"

"That I didn't like it. Because I did. There. Are you happy now?" She crossed her arms and glared at him.

Actually, yes, he was happy to hear about that. He hadn't kissed her since that awkward peck on the lips when they were married, but it was gratifying to hear that she hadn't faked a response.

Or offered it in exchange for fixing a few things on her ship.

"Me, too," he said.

She swiveled her chair back around to face the controls. "So," she said after a pause. She kept her eyes on the starfield.

"So."

"Let me ask you a hypothetical question," she said.

"Go ahead."

"Let's imagine a reality where we weren't forced into an arranged marriage when we were seventeen," she began.

He nodded.

"Let's say you weren't going with me to drop off this accident waiting to happen on a planet in the Outer Rims and I wasn't in trouble with the Fleet. Let's say we met at a bar on Karys Station. What would happen?"

"I don't go trolling around in bars nearly as much as I used to."

"Gods, Kai, just go along with it."

He sighed dramatically. "I'd probably buy you a drink," he admitted.

"And?"

"And what do you want me to say? I think you're really attractive." But *attractive* didn't do Brya justice. He had thought she was gorgeous when they were kids, and he still did. The multicolored hair and tattoos, ordinarily features that didn't catch his interest, only added to it.

"I mean, what would you do after you bought me a drink?"

"Brya, you don't have to go fishing for information. If really you want to know, I don't do one-night stands anymore, and that's what usually happens when a couple meet in a bar, especially on a station like Karys, *especially* with Fleet officers. Can we change the locale? Let's say you were a civilian contractor at Crystal Station and refueled the *Starspot* whenever we stopped by."

"Contractors can't have one-night stands with Fleet officers?"

Damn it, she was enjoying this, and Kai was letting himself get suckered in. "Yes," he said.

"Is that an admission?"

"I'm not discussing that with you, any more than I'd ask you about your old lovers."

She faced him, a smirk on her face. "I don't have as much to tell as you."

"Stop baiting me."

"Stick to the subject and I won't have to. What would you do, if we didn't know each other, and you ran into me in a bar? And don't say you'd ask me to a vidshow or dinner."

"What if those were the things I wanted to do?"

She shot him a look that questioned his intelligence. "Just because I've never dealt with the Fleet until now doesn't mean I don't have a good idea of what goes on in space. There's only so much transporter code one person can write in a day without going bugshit."

She had him there. The Fleet was the reason VD vaccines were widely used. "You really want to know?"

She nodded.

He took a deep breath, but it didn't dissipate the shock flowing through him at the words he was going to say, something he never imagined he would utter to his former wife. "We'd be two strangers in a bar."

She nodded again.

"I'd buy you a drink. And then I'd give you a story about some heroic act I'd done, rescuing a litter of kittens from some evil overlord in the Rims, a bullshit story like that. You would fall for it, and then I'd take you back to my hotel and fuck you senseless."

Brya stared at him, jaw open in shock.

No, he couldn't believe he had said something like that. He winced. "That came out wrong."

She fumbled for words. "No, it didn't. You made your

point." She was blushing furiously, clearly flustered by his admission. Over the last few days, he had seen her far more collected about being chased by a pirate and then a broken fuel line. Yet here she was, her color running high as he told her about what used to be a regular night on shore leave.

He meant every word, and she knew it.

Kai rose from the co-pilot's seat. "I have some stuff to read in my cabin," he said.

She flushed. "It can hardly be called a cabin."

He'd definitely gotten under her skin.

"My room, then. I have an engineering text to read up on. Let me know when we're arriving at that spaceport."

It was true that a fuel line malfunction occurring in this part of space and on a ship like the *Rapture* didn't pose a major threat. Brya could see from the report she kept running and obsessively checking that it was a small leak and they probably could have gone to the Rims before they ran into serious problems. Brya didn't like *probably*. The damaged line helped feed the secondary programs of the ship, like the replicator, communications, and the computer that ran separately from the rest of the primaries. But the connections ran around the cargo bay housing the ungraded fuel she was illegally transporting, and if the leak expanded, it could ignite her shipment. It was better to be safe than sorry, and the repair would set them back only an hour or two. Brya had completed those kinds of fixes before on other ships.

The fuel leak kept Brya's mind off Kai's earlier announcement. She couldn't help but feel flattered and more than a little turned on at what he said. She had been about to propose another hypothetical situation, one closer to reality, but she realized in time that Kai clearly had no intentions of carrying out any of the answers to the questions she had posed.

It was for the best, really. After they had delivered the ungraded fuel to Ishka and Wethmore was taken down, they would go their separate ways. Kai was bound for bigger and better things in the Fleet, and Brya just wanted to try to enjoy her life. It hadn't turned out exactly as she planned, but flying a freighter through the galaxy beat ostracism or abuse on Ralani any day.

There were a few ships in orbit around the Landen Spaceport 201, and she hailed traffic control for clearance. The spaceport resembled a floating narrow tower, twenty decks in all. It was one of the older ones, built when spaceports were just that, and not gigantic artificial worlds like Karys Station "Good evening, gentlemen," she said. "This is Captain Brya Dennir on board the *Rapture*, requesting permission to dock."

"Hello, Captain," said a disembodied voice through her comm panel. "Registration?"

"Still the same. You should have it on file, and I'm flying with my ID."

"You're not broadcasting, Captain."

"Let me check. Maybe there's a glitch." She pulled up the program that controlled ship-to-station communications on her console. There was the *Rapture*'s ID code, set to broadcast in open space. She sighed. "Control, could you check that again? My ship tells me I'm broadcasting my ID. *Rapture*, registered out of Prime in Alliance Space to Brya Dennir, ID F100453896-D." She sighed in irritation. *Great, intership communication's decided to take a nap today. How convenient.*

There was a pause on the other end, followed by muted taps as the traffic controller tried to verify her ID. "No, we're not picking it up."

"Can't you input it manually?"

"We need to see your ID on our screens here, Captain. Standard operating procedure."

"Well, *my* computers are telling me that my ID is broadcasting. Is there any interference on your end?" she said, trying to keep the impatience out of her voice. She needed a favor from the spaceport, after all.

"We're not picking up interference. Your ship is registering as an unknown."

"I've been there before. I still have clearance codes. I can transmit them to you." She brought up the codes that had let her dock at the spaceport before and set them to open broadcast. Her ship's ID would be embedded in the codes.

"Receiving, Captain! Damn it!" yelled the controller. "Cease transmission! Do you want to give away docking codes to everyone in the galaxy? We're not running a charity here! Shit!"

Brya grinned and canceled the broadcast. "Am I cleared for landing, sir?"

"Cleared, Captain Dennir. Don't ever do that again. Do you need a berth or are you going to be leeching off an exterior airlock?"

"I just need a berth to make a couple of repairs myself, two hours tops. Is Zorel running the show today?"

"Yeah, he's here. Transmitting unlock code to you now, Captain. Do you need any help?"

"No, but thanks." Her comm console pinged an incoming transmit, and she downloaded the authorization code to her system. Deck seventeen, berth 89B.

"After that stunt, you wouldn't be likely to get any help anyway," said the traffic controller. Brya grinned again. "Proceed to your assigned berth, Captain."

Brya guided the *Rapture* around a passenger vessel and a few other freighters to the designated airlock. "We're here?"

said a voice from behind her. She started in her seat and turned around to face Kai.

"Yeah."

"There's a problem with your communications?"

"Occasionally. Today was one of those occasions."

"I'll take a look when we're docked," Kai said. Brya opened her mouth to protest, but he continued, "It's my job. Maybe Wethmore did something to it when that fuel was loaded."

That thought had lingered in Brya's mind, too, but she didn't want to think about it. "It's happened before. We'll be in dry dock for only a couple of hours. Just long enough for me to patch that leak and get the hell out."

"It won't take me long to check out a ship this size."

The *Rapture* glided into a landing bay, locking into place in a dock that could hold three freighters. It was one of the cheap docks that required ships' crews to clear the area every time a ship came or went from the spaceport, and the ship parked next to hers had a crew waiting impatiently in the access corridor. As soon as the dock's safety lights flashed from red to green, the corridor's automatic doors unlocked and crew spilled back into the area to work on their ship.

"I'm going to check in and see Zorel," Brya told Kai. "He practically owns the spaceport, and before you ask, I've dealt with him before. Nice guy, but I need you to stay here. He won't want to be involved in this, and I don't want him involved in this."

"Are you going to be safe?"

He was worried about her. It had been a long time since anyone had been, and it touched her. "I'll be fine," she said. She opened a cabinet at the back of the cockpit and took out her toolbox.

"Do you want to take a weapon with you?"

She shook her head. "That won't be necessary. Zorel

would never speak to me again if I turned up in the dock office with a charged rifle, expecting two hours' credit. You never want to piss off the people who help you when you're in a tight spot, you know?" She entered a code on the console near the ramp's exit. "Go hide." She pressed her palm into the console and the entrance ramp unlocked with a hydraulic hiss. Kai nodded and headed through the living area's doorway.

She was greeted with a rush of chilly air. She walked through the corridor outside the dock to the administration office.

She found Zorel sitting behind his desk in his fifteenth-deck office, fiddling with a miniature sensor array that was dwarfed in his hands. He was a big man, middle-aged, his hands perennially stained with engine lubricant, a testament to his willingness to help out a freighter captain in need of an extra body. "Zorel!" Brya said, genuine delight in her voice. A frisson of guilt threaded through Brya at the thought of hiding Kai from him, but it was necessary.

"Dennir! How the hell are you?" He set aside the sensors and walked around the desk to embrace her. "Been too long. Where have you been hiding?"

"Everywhere," she said. "I'm only here for an hour or two. I have a fuel leak."

His bushy brows rose in concern. "Well, shit. Is everyone okay?"

"Yeah, it isn't too bad. I'm on a run to the Rims, so I don't want to take any chances."

"Don't blame you. You paying upfront, or are you going to be making your way through Landen again in the next week or two?"

"I'll see you in a few days," she said. "I don't know exactly how long I'll be in the Rims, so I can't say for sure."

Zorel nodded, accepting her word. "I know you're good for it. Want some help?"

"No, thanks."

"Got time to stop for a beer? I'm buying."

She shook her head. "No, thanks. I'm just in and out tonight."

"Next time you're here, then," said Zorel, unperturbed. "Good to see you, as always."

Brya said her thanks and goodbyes and returned to the *Rapture*. She decoded the exterior cargo bay doors and walked inside, purposefully avoiding looking at the starboard cargo bay door where the petrik was housed. The bay corridor was accessible from the interior of the ship, but she always kept that entrance locked as a safety precaution. There were two smaller portside bays, currently empty, with the boat's maintenance access tunnel entrance between them.

The door to the maintenance tunnel was only waist high, and she had to crouch to open it. Her toolbox was right where she left it the last time something broke, locked to the deck behind the door. She removed a set of disposable coveralls from it and shook them out of their packaging, then slipped them on, taking care to cover her face. She adjusted the material so she could better see out the face covering's clear window. If the leak was worse than she thought, she wouldn't have to worry about burns or inhaling fumes. She shone a flashlight from her toolbox around the narrow space before crawling in on her hands and knees.

She ran a datacorder over the wall closest to the cargo bay. It beeped when it traced the fuel leak. She unscrewed a couple of tiles where the instrument indicated the leak, irritated at how easily they were removed. Was she going to have to replace the tunnels' tiles and fastenings before she could afford to?

There it was. A thick plume of yellow steam lazily crept toward her from a break in the fuel line pipe. It wasn't a catastrophe, but it was definitely worse than the *Rapture*'s computers had indicated. Her eyes widened at the size of the leak. If she had ignored it and pressed on toward the Rim Worlds, they wouldn't have made it more than three or four days before they were stranded in space or worse, the fuel ignited her illegal cargo.

The thought of it reminded her of Dav and her breath sped up in panic. The tunnel felt far too small, like it was running out of air. It took her a moment to collect herself and breathe normally again. "You're getting out of this alive," she whispered, trying to bolster her courage and force away the bad memories.

She peered closer at the slim pipe. The break was clean and straight. Most breaks were irregular, veering off at odd angles and into tiny cracks, usually occurring when a ship was loaded with the incorrect grade of fuel or sometimes by simple by wear and tear. But this was too tidy. She inspected the line, a sinking feeling in her stomach. It looked like it been made deliberately, with a laser.

She crawled back a little to survey the rest of the damage, thoughts whirling through her mind. Someone had done this on purpose. *Wethmore* had done this on purpose.

Her hands shook. She dropped the flashlight. Her thoughts went back to the dockhand at Karys Station, telling her about her pair of visitors while the *Rapture* was in dry dock. Why was he trying to kill her en route to the Rims? She didn't doubt that violence would occur when she made the drop, but she hadn't expected this. It didn't make sense to kill someone being blackmailed.

Brya steeled herself and collected her flashlight. She dug through her toolbox and came up with patches for the fuel line and expertly fused them to the pipe. They melted into it, disappearing at the edges until all that was left was a shiny spot where the new material had taken hold. When she ran a diagnostic on her datacorder, it showed the patches to be effective. The leak was contained.

She crawled out of the maintenance tunnel and stripped off the coveralls, balling them up in her fist. She shoved them through a wall-mounted disposal unit with more force than necessary. Fury swept through her as she stalked through the cargo bay corridor, off her boat to seal the exterior doors, and back up the entrance ramp to the cockpit.

Back on the ship, she booted up a maintenance program and scanned the fuel lines. Like she expected, everything was reported to be running smoothly, but that didn't take the edge off her bad mood. "Kai?" she called.

"Can I come out now?"

"Stay away from the viewports."

The lounge door opened and he crawled to the cockpit on his hands and knees. "Everything okay?" he asked.

"No," she replied curtly, and explained what she had found. He hauled himself to a sitting position on the floor, and listened.

"So it stands to reason there are other things wrong with your ship," he surmised, and she nodded.

"You wouldn't happen to have some kind of military-grade scan programs with you, would you?" she asked.

"Brya, I travel with spare sensors. I'm a little insulted that you think I wouldn't have something as basic as a highly invasive and only technically legal deep-scan program. As a matter of fact, I have two. I have a hard copy of a highly top-secret program in my duffel, and the coding for a blocker on my datapad. If you want me to, I can copy the data to a key and activate the program."

She nodded. "I want to check everything out before we leave the spaceport."

Kai started crawling back to the lounge, but Brya jumped to her feet. "You shouldn't be moving like that in your condition," she chided. He stopped and sat again.

"The program is on a datakey in the front pocket of my duffel," he explained. "My datapad's on the bed."

She found them easily and brought them back to the lounge, along with a spare datakey for him to copy the second program to. "I'm glad we haven't gotten in touch with the Fleet yet. I don't want to until we know for sure that my comms aren't being monitored," she said. The Landen star lane was full of independent communications beacons, and Brya hadn't been assured enough of the Fleet's untraceable channels to check her transmits. She had worked for Wethmore long enough to know that nothing was truly untraceable.

"We really have to check in, you know," Kai pointed out. "But yeah, your paranoia may have worked for the best."

He and Brya went to the control closet off the engine room, where his program could be activated without slowing down the other functions of the ship. He hadn't wanted to access the primaries from the cockpit, explaining he could do a more thorough job if he began at the roots of her controls.

"Now what?" Brya asked him.

"We go back abovedeck and wait for the program to finish. It won't take too long."

They retrieved coffee from the galley panel and their cups were nearly drained when a chime rang throughout the ship. Feeling guilty about the position they were in, Brya crawled on her hands and knees with Kai to the cockpit, where she pulled up the results from the scan. Her eyes widened in shock and a wave of nausea had her gripping the edge of the console.

"A K-Bot!" Her voice came out in a panicked yelp.

"Holy shit," said Kai, and rising on his knees, inspected the report marching across the screen.

"'Holy shit' doesn't begin to cover this. This is a disaster!" Tears sprang to her eyes and she swiped a hand across them. She was going to have to buy a whole new ship.

"I'm sorry," Kai said. Regret and anger laced his words. "If I could remove it, I would."

"So the Fleet hasn't figured out a way to clean a K-Bot off a ship's systems yet? *Fuck*!" Brya lay back in her seat and tried to delay the meltdown she knew she was going to have soon. A K-Bot was the worst kind of malicious software, one that quietly monitored and logged all of an infected ship's computer and communications systems to a remote controller. They were nearly impossible to detect with civilian methods, which explained why it hadn't been picked up when she ran scans before they left Karys Station, nor could it be removed. "At least tell me this one isn't rigged under Wethmore's control and going to blow the *Rapture* out of the star lanes."

Kai was still reading the report. "No," he said. "This is a low-level K-Bot. It just spies on all of your activity."

"Thank the gods we haven't contacted the Fleet yet," said Brya.

"Exactly. But it would have recorded all the repairs I've made to the ship. That's what I'd be worried about— Wethmore figuring out if you have someone else on board. Do you know anything about the repairs I've made? Would Wethmore assume you made them?"

"I haven't worked for him in a couple of years, and I've always been quick to learn new things. He could believe I know how to fix a replicator." Brya thought quickly. "Can you deactivate the K-Bot?"

"This kind, I probably could deactivate certain controls. I'd also have to do a little research first. I'm not sure I'd recommend deactivation anyway, because then Wethmore would know you've found it."

Brya saw the wisdom in that, but it wasn't a consolation. "Do you think we should just ditch the ship and contact someone in the Fleet to pick us up here?" Her heart lurched at the thought. All of her money, her hopes and dreams, were invested in this boat.

"That would be a wise course of action under normal circumstances, but the Fleet really wants to meet up with Wethmore."

She stood up and paced the cockpit. "Couldn't they just ambush him at the rendezvous point? I really wish someone had thought of that earlier."

Kai's reply was patient. "Brya, I've been with the Fleet a long time. Like every business and organization, there are a lot of morons who haven't been in the field in decades and don't understand that things have changed. It would be safer if they just ambushed him, yes, but they have to actually catch him accepting illegal fuel. There's also that deal you made with them." She snorted, but he grabbed her leg as she tried to walk past. "They won't keep you out of jail if you don't go along with this. As much as it pains me and scares the shit out of me to say this, we *have* to stay on this ship. I know enough about K-Bots to tell you that this one isn't designed to kill us. It's just monitoring your computer activities. There isn't a recording device logging all spoken conversations. There isn't an explosive built in. The ship is still space-worthy until we get to Ishka."

"How are we going to get in touch with the Fleet then?" She hated the desperation in her voice.

"It'll be a pain in the ass and I'll have to bastardize my datapad, but I can probably rig a portable communication system on it and use the untraceable channels independently of your ship," he said. "I've done it before. The signals will be a little off once we leave Alliance space, but it'll still work."

"What about my ship?" she said. "I can't use this thing anymore once this mission is done."

"The computer systems can be overhauled and replaced."

"Do you think I have that kind of money? It'll be cheaper

to buy a new boat. I can't afford that, either." She sank into the captain's chair, hands covering her face. "This just keeps getting worse and worse."

"Brya, we don't know what will happen when we meet up with the Fleet," Kai said gently. "They might have to impound your ship anyway, because of the fuel."

"But I would get her back eventually!" she said. "I know she's not much, but she's *mine*. This is my home and livelihood. It's not easy, but I like what I do." She lowered her hands, twisted them in her lap, and looked away. "I'll have to pilot for a shipping company." There went her dreams of independence.

Kai nodded, regret in his eyes. "If I could, I'd fix everything for you," he said.

"No, you wouldn't. I won't let you." As devastated as she was by the impending loss of her ship, she refused to allow him to spend that kind of money and time on it when he'd done so much already. When she had treated him terribly for years. She turned to the controls and keyed in a course for Ishka. "Let's go."

CHAPTER 8

Kai and Brya traveled in peace for a couple of days, the K-Bot never far from their minds. True to his word, Kai turned his datapad into a makeshift transmitter and could finally touch base with Captain Setroff on the *Starspot*. Datapad in hand, he perched on the side of the bed at the scratchy visual of his commanding officer.

The reception was spotty and there was a delay when they spoke, but Kai managed to convey to his commanding officer that their situation was direr than previously thought. "Brya has suggested that the Fleet simply take over," he said when he finished. "She's terrified of the K-Bot."

"The Fleet won't look at it that way," Setroff said. "Remember her deal."

"Yeah, I reminded her of that, too."

"It would be reasonable of them to take over the mission and work out a plea bargain, maybe have her spend a few months on a minimum security prison colony instead. But we're dealing with Admiral Falta." Setroff paused for a moment, obviously trying to not let himself get worked up and go off on a tangent. Neither was sure how long their session could last on Kai's datapad.

Kai shook his head. "I really don't think she deserves prison. She's done some stupid things, but a lot of them were under duress."

"Duress isn't always an acceptable defense in the Alliance, Lieutenant. You know that. And the Fleet is banking on the fact that we've used civilian bait in these situations before. Granted, the civilians were more experienced and working in crews, but they're not looking at things like that. The admiral and Fleet want results as soon as possible. You know how black and white the military is."

Kai knew. He nodded in response, not wanting to go off on a tangent.

"I'll report the K-Bot to Admiral Falta and get his opinion," Setroff said. He sounded stiff, his manner halting, as if there was more to what he wanted to say but couldn't.

Kai hesitated before saying, "Private channel, Captain. You can tell me what you really think will happen."

Now it was Setroff's turn to pause as he searched for words, not wanting to divulge more than he was permitted. "Well, technically I shouldn't, since you're a subordinate," the captain said. "I doubt Falta is going to do anything even if he knows the damage K-Bots do, and we both know that the Fleet isn't going to surprise Captain Dennir with a new freighter or cover her ship's repair costs."

"I figured as much. She's planning on returning to the corporate shipping business when this is over."

"I don't think she's going to prison. I think the Fleet is going to make an example of Wethmore and she'll be able to resume her life."

A knot of tension he'd been holding for days unwound itself. Kai noisily exhaled in relief. "Thank all the gods."

In a rare moment of sensitivity, Setroff asked, "How is she faring personally, Lieutenant?"

Their aborted middle-of-the-night encounter flashed

through Kai's mind, and with it, a corresponding ache around his heart. He doubted the captain wanted to hear that. "Very well for someone who's losing her home, her job, and is being blackmailed," he said finally. "A-okay. She's furious about the damage to her ship, but we're on course for Ishka and I've fixed the onboard replicator and water distribution systems."

"And you?"

"Reading up on some engineering theory," Kai said. "I'm putting in another transfer request when I get back to the *Starspot*."

"You've been putting in transfer requests since you left the academy."

"I'm not really suited to communications."

"If you'd quit goofing off, maybe you would get that transfer already. The Fleet doesn't look kindly on officers who reprogram bots into a choreographed dance. They tend not to trust those people with energy reactors."

"First, I don't want to work with an energy reactor, I want to program. And second, I did them a favor with those cargo bots," Kai said. "All I did was demonstrate a vulnerability in their programming that made the bots vulnerable to remote access in a fun and humorous manner. Besides, you've seen my programming work with the comm badge channel and transporter code. I'm being wasted in communications."

"I'm not saying I disagree with you, and I'll write another recommendation for your transfer if you decide to re-enlist." Setroff steered the conversation back to the mission. "We'll be reaching the Rims by the military lanes," he said. Those star lanes were heavily guarded, with fortified Fleet-controlled spaceports along the way.

"Isn't that a little obvious?"

"We doubt anyone will be keeping close tabs on the military lanes. We're free to move until we're ready to ambush Wethmore. The crew is getting a little antsy, actually. They're not used to not having anything to do, especially since you're not around to liven things up a bit."

Kai doubted that, particularly since he had been on his best behavior most of the time since his transfer to the *Starspot*. That ship's crew was a lot more serious and straitlaced than Kai was used to. "My apologies for not being there to hack into the porn stash security maintains," he said.

It took a few seconds for his words to reach Setroff. "Porn stash? What porn stash?"

Kai smiled and flicked the side of his datapad with his fingernail. "I'll tweak this a little more, and get rid of the delays," he said.

"Damn it, Toric…"

"Console two, in a file with code Ensign Bavel was playing with a few months ago. The name is something with 'Modded' in it, with his initials."

"I don't like to see time wasted, Lieutenant," Setroff said.

"I know you don't, which is why I'm telling you. According to our coordinates, we should both be in approximately the same area within the next seventy-two hours, right, Captain?"

"Correct, and I was also referring to the contraband you've just told me about."

They signed off, and Kai was still smirking a little when he flipped the datapad over and pried off its backing. He made a few minute adjustments with a pair of sonic tweezers, hoping to eliminate the delay in transmits.

"How was it?" Brya asked from the doorway.

He looked up. She looked a little more relaxed today, and the last two nights hadn't roused him from sleep from one of her nightmares, but he could still see the tension in her face, around her eyes. He felt something within himself search her, involuntarily looking for an aura. He had found himself doing that on occasion back on the *Starspot* in recent years, but it was more pronounced around Brya. Based on his limited knowledge of mind talents, he guessed it was because she was a fellow Ralanian. It felt like he was groping around in a darkened room for a light panel and couldn't find it.

"My commanding officer is pretty sure you won't be going to a prison colony when this is over," Kai said, knowing the news would please her.

Her eyes widened and her lips parted in shock. "Really?"

"Nothing is official yet and I'm not supposed to know, but I couldn't let you go on worrying about a prison sentence. If we stick to the plan, you'll be free to go back to your life after Wethmore's picked up. The Fleet's on course for the Rims with the same ETA we have. What does it look like out there?"

"We'll be out of the Landen lane in about an hour, and then we have to divert from the hypergate at the end," she said. "I told you my hyperspace engine is on the fritz. If it weren't, we could be in Ishka's vicinity in less than twelve hours."

"Will you need any help getting around the gate?"

She shook her head. "No, I've traveled this lane plenty of times. It's an easy diversion."

"How's the fuel line?"

"Everything's fine, Kai. I know what I'm doing," she said. "Except for the K-Bot."

Now he saw and felt it. The worry over her ship and its impending loss. Her frustration and anger rippled around the room in palpable waves. He blinked.

"Are you okay?"

"Yeah, I think so. I just felt something."

She sucked in a harsh breath. "Shit. I didn't." She looked at the deck, as though she expected to hear a rumble from the engine below.

"Not that. I felt you. In my head."

Relief suffused her face, and with it, her waves of negative emotion shimmered into something pleasant and peaceful. "Like a telepath."

"No," he said. "Like an empath. Usually I don't pick up what you're feeling, unless it's really strong. You weren't upset, but I could sense your unease over all of this, and then when I told you I didn't feel something about to erupt on board, it... dissolved. That's the only way to describe it."

She arched an eyebrow at him. "Maybe you're a late bloomer."

"While that's a possibility, my theory is that it's because you're also from Ralani."

"But I'm not a telepath or empath."

He shrugged. "It's all I've got to go on. I'm thinking it's an origins-based thing. I can hardly pick up anything from Earthers or their descendants. I don't do too badly with Kalifrans or Saatis." They were the only large group of people with mind talents in the Alliance, and he could only faintly pick up auras from them. "You're the only person from Ralani I've known since I've been in the Alliance."

She sidled into the room and sat at the foot of the bed, across from him. "I don't know anyone who actually grew up on Earth."

"I've met a few," he said. "Most of them don't stick around Earth unless they work in the shipyards. It's too hot and there's too little space."

"Have you been there?"

"No, I've only heard stories from one of the navigators on the *Starspot*. She grew up in a shipyard family."

"She?" She looked at her hands, avoiding his eyes, and while Kai couldn't detect any emotion with his empathic sense, he knew she was curious. Maybe a little jealous?

"She's just my friend," he said to reassure her. Why was he doing that? He and Brya had made it perfectly clear to one another that nothing that wasn't platonic would transpire between them. "Why do you ask?"

"Just wondering."

"What else do you want to know?"

"Nothing right now. I'm sure I'll think of something."

He wanted to tell her that there was no one special in his life at the moment, but what would that have accomplished? Both had made it perfectly clear that nothing but a professional relationship could transpire between them, something he was already regretting. In fact, he already almost wished he hadn't agreed to this mission, just so he would have an innocent excuse to start something with her.

She searched his face. "Is something wrong?"

Yes, something was definitely wrong. He was still the awkward, lovestruck teenager in her presence, only he'd had a few years to learn to hide his feelings. He paused, unsure how to answer without telling her what was really on his mind and further fucking up everything between them.

"No," he said when he found his voice. "Just thinking." She was wearing a sleeveless red t-shirt today, exposing more sparkly tattoos. The work was well-done, but there was a blurry spot on the inside of her left forearm and he focused on it. A large, intricate black rose had been inked on the area, but it was obscuring something. He touched it and she started a little. "What's this?"

"Just a flower I saw in a gardening holo-catalogue when I was looking for ideas for new tattoos."

"What's underneath it?"

"Oh. That. It was Dav's name at one point," she said. "He had mine tattooed on his arm, too, and when I left Wethmore's freighter I had it covered up by a guy I met on Prime. We were sharing an apartment in employee housing, and he tattooed on the side for extra credits. It was cheaper than removal, and besides, the original was done the old-fashioned way, with needles and ink. *Way* too expensive to remove, even if I could find someone who knew how to."

The mention of needles made Kai flinch, along with the revelation that she'd lived with someone. It shouldn't, since he was sure three laser strikes to the leg and wrist were probably more painful and the gods knew he hadn't been a monk since they parted ways. "He?" he said, echoing her earlier question in a single word.

"Yes, *he*, and we were roommates for a while."

That set his mind at ease, somewhat. There was still the matter of her tattoos. "Why the hell would you do that with needles instead of a laser?"

"We were on a freighter when we had them done, and those were the supplies at hand. Come on, it didn't hurt *that* much." She smiled. "If it puts you more at ease, everything else was done with a laser. That only tickles a little. You've never had anything done?"

He shook his head. "Not my style, I'm afraid." He turned her arm slightly to look at the tattooed stars gracing her skin in irregular loops. They were done in iridescent gold and silver and shimmered under the cabin lights. "Is this a constellation or something?" he asked.

"No, I just wanted stars there. Almost all of them are just things I wanted, without any reasons behind them. Mostly flowers and stars. You know, girly stuff." She smiled, turned her head, and pushed down one of her shirt's straps to reveal the pink and gold vine roses emblazoned on her shoulder. "I always liked these," she said. "They grew up the side of the wall of our house on Ralani, remember?"

He did. He didn't mind them, but he recalled that a lot of people considered vine roses weeds.

"I have blue Abela daisies here," she said, moving on the bed so he could see her other side. The delicate design crept over her shoulder down her upper arm, the small flowers blooming along trailing green vines speckled with tiny leaves. "During my second year with Wethmore, we stopped at a spaceport in the Outer Rims for a few days. There was a great body mod shop there and I went overboard." Kai's breath hitched when she lifted her t-shirt up to reveal a wide swath of black and purple stars decorating her side. They extended past her clothing, disappearing under the waistband of her black pants.

"Huh," was all he could manage.

She readjusted her clothing and stood up. His empathic sense started reaching out of its own accord but detected nothing, so he guessed she wasn't deliberately trying to torture him. He forced his expression to remain neutral. "They're beautiful." *Damn.* That didn't come out right. He tried again. "Very well done."

"I really look like a pirate, don't I?" she said, a teasing lilt to her voice.

She looked nothing like the pirates he'd seen during his Fleet career. He was about to tell her that, but stopped himself in time, unsure how that would be received. "You look like a nice pirate," he finally said.

"I see." She eyed him one last time, and he couldn't read her expression or aura. "I'm going to check on the Landen exit."

There wasn't much to do to get out of the star lane. Brya just had to ignore her ship's hypergate warning and avoid getting sucked into it. The gate here had a weak pull, another one of Landen's perks. She plotted a short course around the entrance to hyperspace and transferred the *Rapture* to the Packer lane, one of the original trading routes. They passed a communications beacon and she downloaded a traffic report.

There was nothing surprising in it, just the usual boats in transit, including Renascent Galactic freighters, a small Fleet patrol ship, and a couple of independent ships whose captains she was acquainted with, nothing nefarious. She always picked Packer coming out of Landen because it was a legal lane. The Fleet presence strongly discouraged smugglers and pirates.

While she technically fell into that category with the cargo she was currently carrying, she wasn't going to dwell on it. She had every faith that if for some strange reason the Fleet hailed her, she would be allowed to go on her way. If she couldn't, that just meant they had lost an opportunity to get a boil on the ass of the galaxy on a prison colony. It came down to traveling through unregulated stretches of dead space without worrying about the Fleet, or taking a safe route and risking being busted for illegal cargo she was sanctioned to move. It was an easy choice to make.

It didn't take much concentration to navigate her ship into the Packer lane, and she could turn the controls over to autopilot and relax if she wanted to. But she stayed in the captain's seat, unsure what to do.

She had been an idiot, showing off her tattoos to a man who probably thought she was trying to tease him. Not just a man, she corrected herself. Her former husband and the man she had tossed away, who she had no right to be interested in. But she hadn't meant to come across that way. He had asked about the work she had done, artwork that she was still delighted to have decorating her body and proud of, and like a Fleet station groupie, she had shown off a lot. She felt herself flush with embarrassment. Meeting Dav at the age she had meant she hadn't had the opportunity to develop the man-eater skills other women her age possessed.

If she had them, she would know what to do about Kai. She knew what she wanted, but she had no idea how to go about it and had already resigned herself to the reality that nothing could happen. He was still Kai, but he was with the Fleet. Fleet officers didn't take up with former smugglers and current small-time freighter operators.

She sighed and turned back to the navigation console in front of her. It was less than three days before they reached Ishka. The final twenty-four hours would require her to be on full alert. They were heading into an area with unregulated traffic and sparsely patrolled by the Fleet. For the first time, she wished the *Rapture* was equipped with a full weapons array.

Sad and frustrated, Brya leaned back in the captain's seat. She didn't know until now that it was possible to be lonelier working with someone than alone.

CHAPTER 9

A red alert siren erupting through the ship roused Brya from sleep, and she bolted out of bed and dashed for the cockpit. Her bare feet slapped against the deck's cold tiles and her heart pounded as she slid into the captain's seat. She didn't have to check the computer's reports to see what the problem was: it was staring at her through the forward viewport.

A gigantic cluster of space junk loomed dead ahead, about ten minutes away at the speed the *Rapture* was traveling. It shimmered against the black backdrop of space and stars, highlighting hard, bright green and yellow clumps that indicated used fuel waste.

She had been roused out of bed by a pile of garbage.

She felt her panic ebb away, and she almost laughed in her relief. She altered the ship's course slightly to avoid a collision, and silenced the alarms. Then she opened the messages waiting for her on the navigation console, a generic one sent out to all ships in the Packer lane in the garbage's vicinity. It was sent out by a Fleet ship patrolling the lane and had prompted the red alert. The *Rapture* was set to issue a less ominous yellow alert at sensing anything large and cumbersome in her way, like garbage or an asteroid, and wouldn't have sent her scrambling out of bed at—she checked the time. Two-forty in the morning. "For fuck's sake," she muttered.

Illegal dumping wasn't much of a problem in the big star lanes shared by transport and commercial traffic, especially when they were as heavily patrolled as the Packer lane. Someone thought they were being smart and could avoid disposal fees at a spaceport by jettisoning their waste in the middle of the night. It was the work of an amateur. Any captain worth his ship knew the Fleet never slept, and whoever had dumped their garbage was looking at a hefty fine.

Kai appeared next to her, rubbing sleep out of his eyes. "Is everything okay?"

"*That's* your response to a red alert?"

"I've been through enough false alarms to not get worked up about it. I'm sort of trained to remain calm."

She sighed. "Must be nice."

"*You're* also relaxed and guiding us around whatever that is."

"Used deccarite," she said. "It's a very heavy and very expensive fuel you usually only see on starliners. It costs a hell of a lot more than any grade of petrik. It costs a mint to dispose of, too. And it tends to solidify, as you can see." She gestured to the viewport. A chunk of the fuel sheared off and drifted away. Brya cut a wide berth around it and increased her ship's speed to get away. According to the ship's computers, a pair of Alliance Fleet shuttles were already flying to the debris to collect samples and figure out where it came from.

The space junk behind them, Brya reset the course along the lane and the ship's systems back to night. The lights dimmed in an imitation of night on a planet, the settings Brya preferred. Light panels inset near the floor gave off a warm, familiar glow as she and Kai returned to the living area. "I'm not going to get back to sleep any time soon. Do you want some tea?" she asked. "It's proper tea, not replicated." She opened a cupboard and removed a tin of loose leaves, then boiled water at the replicator. She doubted she'd be getting back to sleep right away, so she might as well enjoy a nice cup.

"Please," said Kai, and he sat down at the table.

Brya felt him watching her as she prepared the tea in a small china pot, part of an antique set she had found at a market on Prime and one of her most cherished possessions. Finally, she set the teapot and a pair of matching cups and saucers on the table and poured cups for both of them. "I don't have any milk," she said. "I think I have some honey somewhere though, if you want it."

He shook his head. "No, thank you."

They sat across from one another, knees touching. There was a comfortable silence surrounding them, and Brya felt a sense of peace for the first time in years. Right now it was easy to pretend there wasn't an angry pirate after her, the Fleet wasn't waiting to throw her in jail if she didn't cooperate with his takedown, and she didn't have worries about how she was going to make a living when this whole episode was over. That Kai wasn't going to walk out of her life in a week's time. She ached at the thought, and her mood darkened. She sipped her tea thoughtfully.

She wished she could do everything over again. It wasn't the first time she had ruminated on the series of mistakes her life was, but it was the first time she wished Kai had been a part of her starting over in the Alliance. She should have given themselves a chance when they still could.

Kai broke the silence. "What are you thinking about?"

She smiled over the rim of her cup. "You can't tell?"

He shook his head.

"Nothing," she lied. "You?"

"Me neither."

She wanted to know what it would feel like to have his hands, his mouth on her body, and again her thought drifted back to the night she woke him up with her dreaming. She barely suppressed a shiver.

Kai shifted in his seat. Had he picked that up? She tried to think about kittens, the flowers at their house on Ralani, her busted hyperdrive engine, anything but what it felt like to fool around with him in her galley.

Fool around. She stifled a giggle at the terminology.

He caught her eye and lifted a brow. Maybe he had picked that up.

She found herself wanting him to. Brya knew he wanted her and he had admitted as much in the cockpit before. Space travel meant there was a lot of time twiddling thumbs, and the gods knew they could be put to better use. She felt her face grow hot, and she smiled.

"What is it?" he asked.

She shook her head, unable to shake her expression.

Kai set down his cup. "You're really bad at hiding things," he said.

"I gathered that the other night."

"Are you talking about my nightmare or what happened after?"

His next words were a little strangled. "You know damn well what I'm talking about, and this is just as difficult for me."

Brya stood up and collected the empty teacups and saucers. She silently rinsed them out and put them away, trying to form a response. The tension in the air was palpable, and she felt a little heady. Finally she said, "Well, what do you want to do about it?"

He was frozen in his chair, staring up at her with a feral look in his eyes. Her breath hitched. He looked downright dangerous, like an animal about to pounce.

"Don't pretend you don't know," he said. His voice was

level, but she could pick up an undercurrent of frustration and lust.

"I want to hear it from you." Where had that teasing, sultry tone come from? It belonged to a woman in an evening dress and heels, not a barefoot freighter operator in pajamas.

He slowly rose from his seat, his eyes never leaving hers. In the galley's dim light she could see his pupils were dilated, and her heart began to pound so hard she was sure he could hear it.

"I want what I always have." He crossed the short distance between them in a few silent, stealthy steps. Brya backed against the counter, a little apprehensive at the intensity in his face. "Since we were married, since I saw you again, and all the time we spent apart. I want you."

He was so close to her she could see his pulse beating in his throat. When he lowered his head to her ear, she expected he would kiss her, but he didn't. Instead he murmured, "If I start anything with you, I'm not letting you go again. You'll be stuck with me this time. Are you sure you want that?"

You'll be stuck with me this time. The words brought her back to their meeting again at the Karys Station concourse. But the cloud of anxiety she'd been living under since that day evaporated when his lips touched the sensitive spot under her ear. His words and his breath against her skin sent Brya's senses into overdrive. She reached out and curled her arms around his neck, bringing him closer. Still, she was coherent enough to form an honest reply, to not completely ignore the tiny voice of reason in her mind. "Don't ask me for that yet." His body stiffened against hers, and she knew it wasn't from desire. "I want you, and I want this. But I don't know how much more of myself I can give you right now."

His hold on her loosened enough so he could step back. He wore a serious expression. "What do you mean?"

"It means I like you and care about you and we could be totally wrong for each other, but every god of every faith knows I want you." She took a step toward him. "I want you to do to me what you said you wanted to the other night."

"I don't think we're wrong for each other." He moved for her again, but instead of continuing where they had left off seconds before, he collected her in his arms. Her head rested against his shoulder, and she felt his next words rumble though her. "I looked for you for years. I had to know you were all right."

"I was," she said. Technically, it was true.

"No, you weren't. I wish I could have done something to help you."

She framed his head in her hands and kissed him. He responded eagerly, his tongue teasing her lips apart. She let the kiss go on for a moment before she broke away reluctantly. "It's okay now," she said softly. "We're both here now, and we're both alive."

Gods, was she ever aware that both of them were alive. His arousal pressed into her hip, and his hands slid over her body, as though he were memorizing it. Her breath caught when his hands slipped under the hem of her shirt and he skimmed his fingers over the slightly raised flesh where she had been tattooed, callused fingertips whispering over her skin. His touch woke up something inside her that had been long dormant, and she wanted more.

But not in the galley. The memory of what nearly happened the last time they were here in the middle of the night intruded on her mind, and she broke away long enough to grasp his hand and say, "My cabin. *Now*."

She led him the short distance to her cabin, anticipation thrumming through her veins. She couldn't remember the last time she felt like this, if ever. She couldn't suppress a small cry from escaping her when he pressed her against her cabin wall, lips fastened over hers. His hands gripped her hips, pulling her closer to him, the sensation was so intense it sucked the breath from her.

She broke the kiss and murmured against his lips, "Bed."

He pulled away from her, a sly smile blooming across his face. "What, you don't want to get fucked against a wall?" His hands slid down her hips to her thighs, and he hoisted her up so her legs wrapped around his waist.

She squeaked, but didn't resist. "Actually, that sounds hot."

Even though her body was screaming at her to let him have his way with her, she didn't protest when he carried her, body still wrapped around his, to her unmade bed. He set her down gently, an uncharacteristic tenderness despite his crude question. "Next time," he said. Promise laced his voice, and a shiver coursed through Brya's body at his words.

She leaned back against the pillows, levering herself up on her elbows. "But I'm thinking about *this* time, Kai."

He replied with a kiss, nipping at her lower lip with his teeth. Another flare of passion sparked through her, and her hands fisted his well-worn t-shirt, tugging at it, desperate to feel his skin against hers. He helped her with it, shucking it off and tossing it somewhere on the floor, and Brya was able to look her fill for the first time.

All the gods everyone in the universe believed in, Kai was magnificent. His skin nearly glowed in the cabin's dim light, his eyes glazed over with lust, and she knew hers must look the same. She reached out and caressed his stomach, his body trembling at her touch. Her hands traveled lower, over his loose sleep pants and brushing against the hard length of his cock. His breath hitched, and he pushed against her hand, silently urging her on.

Brya wrapped her hand around him, stroking his erection through the fabric. But after a moment, Kai placed his hand over hers, stilling her. "If you keep doing that, it'll be over before it starts." This time, it was his turn to pluck at her ratty pajama top. "Take this off."

"You don't find my choice of lingerie alluring?"

"No, seeing you naked is alluring. Take it off."

She bit back a smile and pulled her top over her head. A groan of appreciation rose in Kai's throat at the sight of her. His fingertips traced the outline of her collarbones, the feather-light touch sending a frisson of heat through her. They drifted across her skin, over the tips of sensitized breasts, down to her navel. "What are you doing?" she whispered.

"Memorizing you."

Maybe Kai understood now how uncertain she felt about their future, or the lack of it. It was an ugly, sobering thought, and Brya pushed it away.

They had tonight, and that would have to be enough for now.

She locked her hands around his neck and brought his face to hers for a kiss. Her hips rose up of their own accord to meet his, his body thrusting against hers in a poor imitation of what both of them wanted. His lips traveled down her jaw and neck, until they caught one stiffened nipple in his mouth. Brya whimpered, wanting more.

Her response ignited something in him, because he became more frantic, tugging her pajama pants down her legs. Before she could help him with his, he was already stripping them off, and he sat up, legs tucked under him, resting on his heels.

She already missed the press of his warm skin against hers. "What is it?"

There was an appreciative gleam in his eyes as he raked her from head to toe. Every scar, every tattoo. "Nothing. Everything's perfect."

If it was possible to blush all over, Brya thought she was doing that right now.

"I think I can feel you in my head right now," he said. "It's intense. That's never happened before."

Brya couldn't claim likewise. Instead, she ran her hands over his bare skin: his muscled thighs, taut stomach, deliberately avoiding his cock. The Fleet kept their personnel in good shape.

She took his hands, pulling him toward her until he moved from his sitting position and his body settled over hers. "I don't want any more foreplay," she whispered.

"Next time?" His erection pressed heavily against her hip. He shifted and she parted her legs, letting him settle between them.

"I thought you were going to fuck me against a wall next time."

"Okay, that can be the third time."

And if there isn't a second or third time? That doubt reared its head again, and she closed her eyes, willing it away.

"Brya?" Kai's voice was a little wary. "Everything all right?"

She swallowed and laced her fingers through Kai's. "Yes," she said. "I want this night with you."

She could tell by the lift of his eyebrow that her meaning wasn't lost on him, but he didn't move away. Instead, he lightly bit at the delicate skin on her neck. "I'll try my best not to disappoint you."

His cock probed at her entrance, eliciting a gasp from her. "I don't think you could."

He pushed further, far too slowly for Brya's liking. "Kai," she said, her voice a strangled whisper. "I need more than that."

Beads of sweat popped up along Kai's brow, but he wordlessly complied until he was fully seated within her.

Oh, gods. This could very well be the best feeling in the galaxy, if not the universe, and it finally hit Brya how much she needed this, needed Kai.

Needing him, or anyone else, scared her, but she wouldn't let that fear spoil her night with him.

She lifted her hips, urging him on, until he took mercy on her and started to move. Like he could read her mind—and by this point, maybe Kai could—he knew exactly what rhythm she wanted, how fast or hard she wanted him to go, and she enjoyed every second of it.

It was as if they were made for each other.

Her nails scored his shoulders, heels digging into his lower back, as he thrust into her. She could already feel her climax building—when was the last time *that* happened?—and she welcomed it, her body already stiffening and clenching around his.

"Brya?" Kai's voice was ragged in her ear. "Tell me what you want."

She tried and failed to form a coherent reply and instead pulled his face to hers for a fierce kiss.

He took that as a good sign, and his intensity increased until she came with a harsh cry against his mouth. Mercifully, he didn't stop, but continued his pace until she felt his muscles bunch up under her hands, could feel the tension in his spine. "Oh, gods, *Brya*..."

His body stiffened against hers and she felt his own orgasm as acutely as her own. Both of them lay still for a moment, the only sounds in the cabin being their breathing and the omnipresent rumble of the ship's engines.

Finally, he pulled out of her and rolled over on his side, taking her with him in his arms. He pressed a kiss to her forehead, and she snuggled closer to him. "Brya," he said, "whatever happens, that was worth it."

Brya checked the time: just after six in the morning. She looked over her shoulder at the naked man sleeping peacefully next to her and slipped out of bed, taking care not to wake him. She pulled an oversized t-shirt over her head before leaving her cabin, closing the door behind her.

They were down to less than forty-eight hours before meeting up with Wethmore. Her stomach knotted on itself and she wished heartily for a drink despite the early hour. Instead, she went to the galley and reheated her forgotten tea from the middle of the night. She sat down at the small table and sipped it without tasting.

Forty-eight hours and the ungraded fuel would be off her ship. Another few days after that and she would be back in Alliance space, looking for work after selling the *Rapture* for scrap. Angry tears pushed at the backs of her eyes and she blinked them away.

There was no point in crying about it. She would start over yet again and in a few years buy another freighter and re-build her shipping contacts. A simple enough plan, but not easy. To lose everything so quickly...

A tear slid down her cheek. She *was* going to lose everything again, including Kai. She looked over her shoulder at the corridor that led to her cabin, unsure how he fit into her life. She wasn't completely clueless, as a teenager or now. She'd suspected long before they left for Alliance territory that he'd nursed a crush on her, and he'd mentioned before that he'd spent years looking for her. Until just a few days ago, he'd always been her friend and now she wanted more. So did he, but in the cold reality of daytime, or what passed for daytime in deep space, she didn't know how their lives would be compatible.

They weren't, really. And now they had to fuck up everything even more by sleeping together. Despite his earlier assertions to the contrary, he would undoubtedly think it happened because she felt she had to and not because she wanted to, or that she was taking advantage of him when she wasn't.

Sex made everything so much more complicated, especially when it was with someone she was already falling in love with. Brya was bad at relationships.

The Alliance Fleet would arrest Wethmore and everyone would return to their normal lives. Except her. She had to create a new normal. *Again*.

She heard her cabin door open and the slap of bare feet against the deck. Kai appeared in the galley doorway, a pair of loose drawstring pants hanging from his narrow hips. He yawned. "Why are you awake at this ungodly hour?"

"Why aren't *you* still in bed?" She kept her voice as level as she could, trying to hide the tears there. She took a hasty sip of tea.

"Because you aren't there."

Well, why did he have to go ahead and say that? Brya felt a fresh wave of tears build behind her eyes and she blinked them away, an action that Kai didn't miss.

"What's wrong?" He slid into the seat next to her, concern etched across his features.

"Besides facing someone who wants to kill me and losing my ship?" And losing him, too, but she didn't add that. "Nothing, Kai."

He wrapped his arms around her. She leaned into him, needing the contact. "I told you I'd help you."

But accepting his help was too much to ask of him, and she knew he wouldn't take no for an answer. Gods, she'd screwed this up so much. But instead of saying so, she wiped at her eyes and let herself relish his warmth.

CHAPTER 10

Ishka had a single spaceport that ushered in the *Rapture* without even bothering to issue docking clearance, which immediately set Brya and Kai on edge. Brya prayed that the Fleet was already there, that there hadn't been a delay on their end and she wasn't going to have to face Wethmore alone.

She was unarmed and untrained in combat, and even though Kai kept assuring her that she wasn't in this alone, she still felt very lost. She'd never done much in the way of face-to-face negotiations when she worked with Wethmore and felt woefully unprepared.

A message appeared in her inbox as soon as the *Rapture* reached Ishka's orbit and passed a guidance beacon, unsigned and from a disposable transmit address, but she knew who it was from. *Dock dirtside, berth 4F, disable engines and cargo bay locks. Leave the ship without weapons, proceed to the café at spaceport and wait. Failure to heed orders will result in consequences.*

Kai read the message over her shoulder, his tablet in hand as he made contact with his superiors. "The Fleet will be there," he said firmly. "You won't do this alone."

"Where will you be?"

His voice was grim but determined. "Hiding out. I'll be armed. I've been in touch with the Fleet. There are already officers ready to act as soon as you follow these orders from Wethmore. They came in on civilian shuttles according to the last comm I picked up."

She nodded and waited for instructions from transit control. A bored-sounding voice crackled through the cockpit speakers. "Power down any weapons and engage heavy-air engines."

"You might want to sit down and strap in somewhere," she told Kai. "How often are you onboard a ship docking planetside?"

"Not much." But he sat down in the copilot's seat, strapping himself in and bracing for the onslaught of gravity.

"Sucks to be you." But not as much as her. Despite her flippant words, her whole body felt like it was tied up in knots at the prospect of seeing Wethmore again, even though Kai kept assuring her she would be fine. "As soon as we land, you hide, no matter how much you might want to puke, all right?"

"Got it. I will try my best not to throw up on your deck."

"I appreciate that." The controls lit up as the *Rapture*'s computers warned her about their impending date with Ishka's atmosphere and recommended activating her heavy-air engines. "Of course," Brya said under her breath. "How stupid do you think I am?" Well, besides getting caught up in a life of piracy and smuggling, but at least she was trying to get out of that life.

The ship vibrated and shuddered as the heavy-air engines stuttered on, and Brya immediately felt the hard pull of the planet's gravity as they began their descent. Even though she'd done this before many times, every muscle in her body still tensed in protest.

The *Rapture* handled heavy air with all the finesse of a meteor falling from the sky. A surprised yelp escaped from Kai as the *Rapture* began what felt like a freewheeling hurtle planetside, but Brya compensated for that, activating manual controls and steering the ship to the docks the computer told her were directly below them. She sneaked a glance at Kai, who gripped the seat armrests and was visibly sweating.

"What the *fuck*?" He slowly released his death grip on the seat and swiped a hand over his sweaty brow. "Is that *normal*?"

"On a freighter, yeah. Was this your first time breaking atmosphere on a forty-year-old freighter, Kai?"

"I—yes. It was."

Her mirth faded as she remembered what was ahead of them. "You need to hide now," she said, damning the tremor of fear in her voice. She shut off the *Rapture*'s engines and entered the codes to unlock the cargo bay. She unsnapped her safety straps and stood up on shaky legs, then took a deep breath. "I'm going to the spaceport's café." She hoped she could find it in time.

She felt like crying. This exchange meant her life with Wethmore was truly and finally over.

It meant her ship was nothing more than a flying scrap heap.

She would have to leave Kai behind, again.

Kai stood up from his seat, all trace of his discomfort at the landing gone. He put a proprietary hand on her arm, stopping her from leaving the cockpit. His lavender eyes met hers, and she shivered at the intensity there. Despite the danger she was about to place herself in, desire unfurled in her, a reminder of all the flirting and teasing they shared on this journey, of their single night together.

"You're going to get through this," he said. "You made it this far on your own, and you'll keep doing it."

You. You made it this far, and *you'll* keep doing this. There wasn't a *we* in there, and Brya completely understood why, even though she didn't like it.

A soldier and destitute spacer would never work out. They both knew that.

Still, she stood up to kiss his cheek, but he caught her face in his hands and planted a heady kiss on her lips that forced all reason from her mind. Her arms slid around his neck and she responded eagerly, leaning into him, needing and wanting more.

It was all of Kai she wanted, for the rest of her life. For a few brief seconds, she let herself imagine that it could happen.

The feeling quickly evaporated when the computer pinged another incoming message, undoubtedly from Wethmore. "Go hide," she said. How many times had she told him that during their journey?

Kai squeezed her hands and dropped a final kiss to her lips. "I'll be in the maintenance tunnel over the cargo bay."

"Please be careful. Your leg..."

"My leg is fine. I'll be able to get into that maintenance tunnel and stay there without any problems. You'll be fine, too. The Fleet is already in position."

"How will I know who they are?"

"You don't, but that's okay." He traced the outline of her lips with his fingers as if memorizing her features. "Let's do this."

She nodded and reluctantly broke away from him. Her stomach twisted in knots, she opened the message. Unsigned again, from the same disposable transmit address. *Café, fifteen minutes. Do not be late.*

It was time to go.

Ishka's spaceport was sparsely staffed, the building itself dirty and falling apart. The *Rapture* was the only ship she saw docked in this part of the spaceport, but she knew there must be a ship under Wethmore's command nearby to transfer the fuel to. Nervousness churned in her gut as she strode through the docking area to the spaceport's excuse for a commercial sector, but she stood tall, hoping she projected an aura of confidence that she certainly didn't feel.

The Alliance Fleet is here, she reminded herself. *I'm not in this alone.*

It turned out that the café was only a brief walk away from the docks, a pleasant surprise since Brya couldn't find any staff to ask for directions anyway. The café was grimy, a light film of grime covering every available surface, and fully automated. Brya didn't have any money to buy a cup of coffee from one of the replicators anyway, not that she'd want to. The gods only knew the last time the machines' components were cleaned.

There were a few patrons milling around the café, as shoddily attired and disheveled as one might expect a backwater planet spaceport's patrons to be. None of them paid any mind to Brya, who slid into an empty chair in the middle of the café. She drummed her fingers on the tabletop, waiting.

Were Wethmore's men already descending on her ship, taking out the illegal fuel and possibly helping themselves to her personal effects? She didn't doubt they wouldn't do that.

Please let Kai be okay.

That was what was most important. As painful a loss as the inevitable scrapping of the *Rapture* would be, losing Kai to because of Wethmore would be worse. She was dangerously close to falling in love with the man—she thought she might already be—and the ship was ultimately replaceable, as painful as that inevitable loss would be. It would be nothing compared to Kai. She knew she couldn't handle him being killed.

She was going to lose him anyway, but he had to stay alive, she told herself. He needed to continue making Alliance space a better place.

She waited, looking down at her hands. She forced herself to stop tapping the table, avoiding drawing attention to herself, and clenched her fingers together until her knuckles turned white. Where was Wethmore? Had the Fleet had already taken him down?

Deep breath. In, out.

Kai had promised she would be okay. She had to remember that.

A shadow was cast over the table and she looked up to see Wethmore grinning down at her, a demon haloed by the harsh lights blazing from the ceiling. She tried to form a greeting but her tongue felt furry and wouldn't cooperate. A squeak escaped her instead.

Wethmore plunked down in the seat opposite her. There was a distinct bulge at his side that told Brya that he wasn't bound to the no-weapons clause part of their deal. "Good to see you got my messages," he said. "I appreciate that you're on time."

She nodded and cleared her throat until she could speak again. "I trust the shipment was in order?"

"It was."

"Am I free to return to my ship in that case?"

"When I get the signal that everything's been moved, you can go back." He flashed a sinister smile at her, teeth unnaturally white against his lips. His smile was artificial and expensive. The man had always been vain. "Until I get that, we stay here."

Where was the Fleet? Her mind raced with what-ifs and she felt her palms sweat. Shouldn't they have acted by now?

She was fairly certain he wouldn't do anything stupid like blow up the *Rapture* and Ishka's spaceport out of spite.

Wethmore had never been one to embrace destruction for destruction's sake. She tried and failed to make her heart stop beating so rapidly, almost certain that Wethmore could hear it and figure out what was happening.

Or should happen. Where the *hell* was the Fleet?

But there was one more thing she needed to ask him. "My boat," she said. "Why did you install a K-Bot on her?"

Wethmore looked at her blankly. "What the hell are you talking about?"

"The bot that's eating its way through the *Rapture*'s systems right now and can't be uninstalled. I have to scrap her when I get back to Alliance space."

He shook his head and stared at her like she had an extra hand growing out of her head. "Again, no fucking clue what you're talking about."

His handheld beeped, a chirp that echoed in the nearly empty café. Brya jumped in her seat and Wethmore chuckled. His smile disappeared when he looked down at the handheld's message, then glared at her. "Bitch."

His voice was a low growl, and the memory of the night he cut off her fingers rudely intruded, until she remembered something—*someone*—more precious onboard the *Rapture*.

They'd found Kai. Brya thought she might throw up. "I..."

He stood up and reached inside his jacket, removing the pistol she knew he'd been carrying. He aimed it at her head, disregarding the other patrons in the café. She doubted they would care, anyway. "You had *Fleet* onboard your scow?" He said the words with the same tone she'd heard so many times before when she was part of his crew. She squeezed her eyes shut, tears leaking from the corners, hating that his face would be the last thing she saw before he finally killed her.

All the gods in all the heavens, please spare Kai. He deserves that much.

The sharp whine of a laser weapon cut through the air, the beam close enough to singe her ear.

I've been shot!

But that thought evaporated when she heard the heavy thump of a body hitting the floor. She dared to open her eyes, numbness pouring through her at the sight of Wethmore's prone form twitching on the floor's dirty tiles. An unfamiliar man wearing a stained brown shipsuit rushed over to her, the indicator lights on his weapon still glowing green. She immediately shot to her feet, sure she was about to be arrested herself.

Instead, a middle-aged woman appeared beside him, as shabbily attired as he was, a medkit in her hand.

"Is he dead?" Brya asked.

"Nah, just stunned," said the man, holstering his weapon. His own handheld trilled from somewhere on his person, and he removed it from a pocket. "Captain Dennir, I'm Lieutenant Anders, this is Janzen." He nodded at the medic. "Wethmore's lackeys found Lieutenant Toric hanging out in a duct over the cargo bay. He managed to get a message to us at the same time they told Wethmore he was there."

Brya didn't bother trying to hide the panic in her voice. "They found Kai? Is he okay?"

"Other than being pulled out of the duct and getting a kick to the ribs, yeah. He's survived worse." He wrapped a pair of glowing sonicuffs around Wethmore's wrists. A mewl of pain escaped him but the woman slapped a pain patch on him. The pirate immediately stilled, his body slack.

Kai had been injured again, now on her account. "Oh, no!"

Anders's brows lifted in surprise at her reaction. "His ribs heal just fine."

How could they be so relaxed about broken ribs? He was still recovering from three laser strikes to the leg, for the gods' sake! She started to leave the café for the spaceport docks, but the medic placed a hand on her arm, halting her. "Give it a few minutes," she said. "There's a larger crew of officers over there arresting everyone and someone will probably get shot before it's all over."

"But Kai..."

"The lieutenant is a trained officer who can take care of himself," she said firmly. "If he had been grievously injured, I would have been called to the dock." She shot Wethmore a look of pure contempt. "This guy here would have been left cuffed to the table while Anders watched him." She nodded at the officer who shot Wethmore. "We've been in contact with Ishka's authorities and the spaceport employees are cooperating with our investigation. Lieutenant Toric's fine."

Then there was one more question Brya had to ask. "Am I under arrest?"

"I'm a medic, I don't deal with arrests. Anders?" She turned to the other officer.

"There's nothing in my orders that indicates you're to be detained. Once the petrik has been removed from your ship and you file a flight plan with Ishka's transit control, you're free to go."

Brya sagged against the table, relief pouring through her despite the uncertainties ahead. The Fleet had held up their end of the bargain and granted her freedom. She was free to go back to Alliance space. Her life was her own again, possibly for the first time ever.

But it would be a life without the *Rapture* or Kai.

Kai expected Brya to be more relieved than she was when she finally reappeared at the dock. Instead, she looked tired and sad, but she summoned a half-smile when she saw him. "Are you okay?" she asked by way of greeting.

"The bone regenerator's doing its thing. I'm fine."

"How did they find you?"

It was his own fault for assuming that Wethmore and his thugs weren't using equipment more sophisticated than they were. "They scanned for life forms aboard the ship," he said. "It pointed out my hiding spot. I sent a transmit to the ground team to let them know I was discovered, then let myself drop out of the maintenance tunnel so they wouldn't start shooting holes in your cargo bay." His reassurances did little to smooth those creases of worry between her eyes, so he wrapped his arms around her. "One of the guys got a kick in. It wasn't even a hard one. Brya, I'm fine, really."

She didn't relax in his arms, and he felt something shift between them, an almost tangible feeling. "I'm glad to hear that," she said.

"I had your ship refueled for the trip back to Alliance space," he said. "I can't do anything about the K-Bot."

She cut him off. "Did Wethmore have anything to do with that? He said he didn't, but I don't believe him."

"And none of his guys are talking. I'll find out for you, I promise."

She nodded and pulled away from him, not meeting his eyes. "Is that it? Can I leave now? Does the Alliance need anything more from me?"

"They'll be in touch." Why was she being so distant? "Brya, when we get back..."

"We go back to our lives," she said firmly.

Kai felt himself blanch. He waited for her to continue.

She looked away, focusing on something behind him. "Kai, I care about you, I really do. But I don't think there's a future for us in Alliance space. We're too different."

A wave of dizziness flowed over him, and he closed his

eyes, fighting to keep his balance. Not this, not after he'd spent so much time trying to find her. "Brya, I don't care about any of that," he said. "Neither does the Fleet. Not really."

"Kai, I need my independence," she said weakly. She sounded like she was on the verge of tears, like she didn't want this.

"We both know you would have that," he said. "Don't lie to me. I think I deserve more than that."

Her eyes filled with tears but she brushed them away impatiently. "It'll be harder to do this after we've run a relationship into the ground," she said. "It's just best to end it here."

Mindful that they weren't alone in the berth, he kept his reply quiet. "You can't believe that," he said. "I've been looking for you for years."

"Kai..."

"I've been in love with you a long time."

"Kai!" This time the sound of her voice attracted some attention. Lieutenant Anders and another grunt Kai didn't recognize looked their way. Brya glared daggers at them until they turned back to their datapads. "You can't mean that. If you think about it, we hardly even know each other." There was a waver in her tone, like she was trying to convince herself of that fact.

"I can and I do. I'm not ready to throw in the towel just yet."

"Kai, just please do this for me."

"I take it I have to find my own way back to Alliance space, then?"

"At least Fleet ships can travel through hyperspace. You'll be home in a day or two." She stalked toward the *Rapture*, where her cargo bay ramp was still extended. "I can't deal with this, Kai."

She couldn't now, but maybe if he gave her some time, she

might be willing to try to make things work. "Okay," he called after her. "Let me get my stuff."

He followed her up the ramp into the *Rapture*'s belly. He headed straight for his cabin, where the bed was still unmade. He shoved his few belongings into his duffel. He found her in the cockpit, filing a flight plan with Ishka's transit control.

"I mean it, you know," he said. "I love you and I want to make this work."

"Kai." She looked up from her screen. "I'm not going to argue over that with you, but I've been married before, to someone just as different from me as you are." Before he could protest, she continued, "I know you're not Dav. But I still don't think this would work. We're too different. This was the first time we've seen each other in over ten years and I'm not even sure you know the real me, just this fantasy you built up in your head."

"I do know you," he insisted. "You're incredibly strong, brave, resilient. You did what you had to do all this time to survive and you made it."

She offered him a weak half-smile. "You know that I'm doing what I do best, right? Running away?"

"You don't have to do that."

She shook her head. "I do. I need to sort my life out. It's going to take some time to do that."

A flicker of hope flared in Kai's chest at her words. That wasn't an outright rejection. "Can we stay in touch?"

"I don't know if that's a good idea."

He pulled up her contacts list in the ship's computer and added every transmit address he could be reached at. "Any time you need something, no matter how insignificant it might be, contact me," he said. "I'll always help you, no strings attached." He took a deep breath, fortifying himself. "And if you ever change your mind, let me know. I'll be on the first shuttle your way."

"All right." She made a few adjustments to her flight plan before uploading it to transit control's computers. "I'm leaving now."

He had the distinct impression that if he tried to kiss her, he might never hear from her again. He took a few steps back, and the relief on her face tore at him. "I'll see you soon," he promised her.

CHAPTER 11

Brya stared at her handheld. Her bank account balance glowed back at her. She had more money than she had in years, but the numbers displayed there were still bittersweet.

She'd received more than she expected for the *Rapture* at the scrapyard, but that didn't ease the ache in her heart. She'd poured her life and meager savings into that freighter, and to have it all stolen away... she gulped. It wasn't just about the money; it was her independence. Independence she was now losing.

She was hired at Renascent Galactic Shipping and Transport almost immediately when she applied a few days prior, and now she was aboard a shuttle bound for their shipyard on a moon colony smack-dab in the middle of Alliance space. The wages were decent and included room and board, and she now had all of her remaining possessions packed in the same duffel she brought with her when she fled Ralani so many years ago.

Her heart gave another squeeze at the thought of Ralani and consequently, Kai.

He deserved someone better than her. He should have a

partner in life who didn't have a history of using him and running away, no matter how much she loved him now.

A part of her had hoped that she would see Kai again when Wethmore was put on trial, a spectacle she'd had every intention of seeing. But a trial was far off as the Fleet waded through piles of evidence provided by the former pirate's crewmembers and his own files and effects, guaranteeing that it would be weeks before such an event would start. And Brya couldn't bring herself to get in touch with Kai herself, not after the way she brushed him off back on Ishka.

She tried to force all thoughts of Kai out of her mind and failed. She sighed irritably, resting her feet on the duffel in front of her as the shuttle began its descent to the shipyard landing pad. At least she'd stopped crying over him. *Baby steps, Brya.*

But she knew, deep down, that she'd never truly get over losing Kai. She'd just get used to not living without him, and that pain in her heart would become second nature to her.

First Kai, now the *Rapture*.

She had been assigned to a C-class freighter for her first assignment at Renascent, a small boat with a shipment of glassware and cutlery bound for a warehouse on the other side of Alliance space. The information packet sent to her handheld contained the ship security codes and a copy of her flight plan, already uploaded. She'd be taking a shortcut via two hypergates and was scheduled to be back at the shipyard in less than forty-eight hours. She'd be a glorified babysitter, she noted. There was precious little for a captain to do while a ship was in hyperspace.

The company shuttle left her in at the shipyard and she walked through Renascent Galactic's chilly beige-painted corridors to her freighter's berth. The corridor was lined with windows that offered a view of the moon colony, all frozen, gray, and dark where the company's exterior lights couldn't reach. It was one of the most depressing places Brya had ever seen, and that included Ralani and the ship that brought her to Alliance space. At least her home world had sunlight and breathable air. Anyone leaving the safety of the company's buildings would require an EVA suit out there.

She punched in the entry code on the ship's lock and walked in, then tossed her duffel in the single, tiny captain's cabin and checked out the bridge. While even smaller than the *Rapture*, it was still a much newer and more reliable ship, and her pre-flight checks revealed a craft in top shape. Wistfulness gripped her as she thought of the *Rapture*, undoubtedly now in pieces, just like her heart.

A voice crackled from Renascent's transit control over the audio communicator. "Dennir? You ready? Your boat's scheduled for takeoff in fifteen minutes."

She leaned over and replied into the navigation console's speaker. "Dennir here. Yeah, everything looks good. Anything I should know about during the hypergates? I don't think I've taken either of those before." The *Rapture*'s hyperspace engines had died long before she was blackmailed by Wethmore.

"The Larsen gate has a bumpy exit. *Real* bumpy. If you're prone to space sickness, you might want to have a bucket handy. Renascent will shit a brick if you bring a ship back with puke on the deck."

"Thanks for the heads up."

"No problem. Sit tight and wait for your signal to depart."

Brya leaned back in the captain's seat, strapped in, and waited.

"This is fucking crazy, Kai, you know that?"

Kai knew, and didn't care. James Anders—longtime

colleague and friend, and now Brya's defender against Wethmore on Ishka—looked around the *Rapture*'s dust-coated cockpit, disdain across his features. "It's a K-Bot," Anders continued. "Even I know that's a death sentence for a ship, no matter what kind it is."

"Yeah, well, only if the computer system can't be replaced. Which this ship's can be." Kai had had the ship towed to a Fleet-controlled dock right in the center of Alliance space. He was paying through the nose for the *Rapture*'s berth and extra security to ensure the K-Bot didn't multiply and infect the station's computers. Kai was pretty sure someone would find an excuse to space him at a later date if that happened.

"Which brings me to my second point."

"I've already heard it." Anders thought Kai was nuts for installing completely new systems into the forty-year-old freighter. Truthfully, Kai had questioned his own sanity at such an undertaking as well. But it would be worth it to see the look of Brya's face when she saw her old ship repaired, including its hyperspace engines. It turned out that the parts required came pretty cheaply at shipyards, at least on Kai's salary and with his contacts.

"Not the stupid amount of time and money you've spent pouring into Captain Dennir's scow," Anders said. "I mean Captain Dennir herself."

Kai paused, splicer in hand. His reflection stared back at him from the darkened monitor he was installing at the command console. "That's none of your business."

"I know, but..."

"Then stay out of it." He raised his head and stared daggers at Anders.

The other man held up his hands in defeat. "I'm not trying to tell you how to live your life. Just don't be disappointed if she still rejects you."

That thought had occurred to Kai, but it hadn't deterred

him from buying the *Rapture* at the scrapyard. "I'll keep that in mind."

It wasn't just how he felt about Brya that motivated him. It was that she had tried so hard to do right in her life, to do the right thing, and that had been snatched away for reasons beyond her control.

Kai knew that she hadn't wanted to leave him, that she pushed him away because of some kind of weird sense of honor. He'd sensed it, could feel the regret radiating off her and see it in her aura. He would try once more to show her they belonged together, that he didn't care what she'd done in the past.

Wethmore had sworn up and down, both on Ishka and in Fleet custody, that he had nothing to do with the K-Bot installation on the *Rapture*. Kai had managed to get his hands on some of Wethmore's files used in the investigation against him and his band of pirates, and nothing in there indicated that he had ever used malware in his attacks on others. He'd always preferred direct, physical attacks and outright robbery.

So who the hell installed it?

He'd managed to isolate the program and studied it in the safety of his own firewalled system and came up blank. There wasn't a signature in the program nor code that indicated its origins, nothing that indicated why a random, poor freighter captain should have her ship's systems eaten by a malicious piece of software. There wasn't even anything in there to disable the engines or throw life support offline. It was just a random, low-level, but incredibly destructive K-Bot.

What if the *Rapture* wasn't the only infected ship?

He set down the splicer and stood up. "You thinking about what I said?" Anders asked.

"No, something else." He walked through the ship, down her ramp to the berth. Anders followed him.

"Kai, what's up with you?"

"I don't think the K-Bot installation on the *Rapture* was random," he said. "And I believe Wethmore when he said he didn't do it. He isn't that subtle."

"Or smart."

"That, too. I'm going to connect to the Fleet network and do a little research into K-Bot reports."

Anders stared at him, brows knitted together. "You think someone's installing malware on small-time freighters?"

"Yes. Think about it, James. K-Bots are usually designed to cause an explosion or disable life support, something disastrous. They're time bombs. This one wasn't. Why the hell would someone install that kind of program otherwise? For fun?"

Understanding dawned on Anders's face.

"Someone cut her fuel line," Kai said. "That's how she found out about it, after she checked her repair status. Someone wanted her to find it and sell her ship for scrap." Another piece of the puzzle fitted itself together in his head. "And stop doing business on that ship."

"Shipping companies."

That was exactly Kai's thought. He nodded. "I'm going to cross-reference K-Bot attacks on freighters," he said. "And see how many small-time captains sold their ships for scrap and were hired by one of the big companies."

Anders nodded. "The big guys get bankrupt employees who know all the shipping lanes and hypergates, all those shortcuts in Alliance space and beyond and who can't afford to turn down assignments."

"Yeah. And I'm pretty sure Renascent Galactic is going to be the common denominator in all of this." They were the biggest outfit in Alliance territory, absorbing smaller transport companies almost as soon as they started operating and stealing clients if refused buyouts. He recalled one of his earlier conversation with Brya: she'd worked for Angel Transport until that company was bought out by Renascent.

Kai strode through the docks' corridors until he reached the berth his own shuttle was docked in. "You need my help?" asked Anders.

"Can you finish splicing that monitor feed on the *Rapture*?"

"Seriously?"

"Yeah. This won't take long." He palmed the shuttle's lock and its rear door hissed open. "I'm just going to connect to the military network and maybe send out a few transmits. I'll be back there soon."

Anders sighed. "You get all the good assignments."

Kai faced him, not bothering to hide his confusion. "I got shot by a brand new recruit the last time I was on official Fleet business. That's hardly a good assignment. And I'll be flying a desk if the Fleet gets their way." His re-enlistment was coming up soon. He had to decide if he wanted to take what the Fleet offered him for the next years of his life, or walk away.

"Like I said, you get all the good assignments. I'm five years away from retirement, Kai. I *want* to fly a desk."

"You can fly mine when I'm done with this." He walked the short length of the shuttle's corridor to its small cockpit and signed into the military network. "But until then, could you finish that splice?"

CHAPTER 12

Brya halted when she saw the broadcast flashing across the vidscreen in the Crystal Station operator lounge. Everyone else standing around, including those who wore Renascent uniforms like her own, ceased conversation and watched the drama unfolding on the giant screen.

"It has been confirmed that Renascent Galactic Shipping and Transport is under investigation for repeated use of malware on the ships of independent freighter captains," the reporter was saying. "The malware is reported to be K-Bots, banned programs in Alliance space. Thirty-seven cases of sabotaged ships have been confirmed within the last four years, and many of those captains were forced to sell their ships for scrap and seek work with a major shipping company or leave the business altogether."

It took a few seconds for the weight of the newscaster's words to hit Brya.

The *Rapture*. Her whole life had been on that ship, and her employer deliberately destroyed it.

A wave of dizziness washed over Brya, and she closed her eyes to fight it off. When she opened them, she saw the shocked looks of her fellow operators, some of whom had undoubtedly lost their ships to malware.

"Gleda Naith was just arrested," someone announced, holding up a handheld.

Who? Brya's expression must have given away her confusion, because the pilot standing next to her said, "Renascent's CEO."

Oh, damn. This was big.

Whoever delivered the news of Ms. Naith's arrest shouted out, "Who wants to get in on a class-action ass-kicking?"

The lounge exploded in a cacophony of angry voices and sobs. Brya slipped from the room before she could get sucked into chatter about class action lawsuits. Even in the best-case scenario, she was unlikely to see any financial compensation for years, if ever. And it wasn't just about the money, not for her.

Did Kai know? He must, even if he wasn't part of the investigation. She ached to get in touch with him but didn't dare to.

She was all wrong for him and they both knew that. Contacting him would only lead to more heartache.

She realized as she walked through Crystal's corridors that she didn't really have a destination in mind. Should she return to the ship Renascent assigned her to? Leave their freighter here for them to deal with and hop on a transport shuttle back to one of the Alliance's inner worlds? She paused and leaned against the corridor's cool wall and closed her eyes, trying to think of a plan.

She might as well take the freighter back to Renascent's headquarters, then find a ride back to Prime. She had no idea if she would be responsible for the freighter if she left it at Crystal Station and it was damaged, and judging by the angry shouts from the lounge that she could hear in the corridor, vandalism was a possibility. Or riots.

It was best to leave before a war broke out between the Renascent operators and station staff. It was a Renascent-controlled station as of six months ago, and people were pissed off.

Brya hurried through the corridor to the station's docks, relieved to see no one there except transit controllers in their fortified booths. She let herself on to her freighter and checked in with them, uploading a flight plan back to the Renascent's moon base.

The transit controller's voice crackled through the cockpit speakers. "All departures are delayed," he said. "The moon's locked down."

"Seriously?" Brya launched the freighter's automatic pre-flight checklist. Life support and fuel were optimal. Her latest shipment, this one of antigrav tools, had been offloaded and the manifest signed by Crystal's foreman. There was no reason she should be detained.

"I don't know if you know this, but Gleda Naith's been arrested."

"I heard." Truthfully, Brya hadn't known nor cared about Renascent's CEO until news broke of her arrest. "And I don't know if *you* know this, but every pilot in the lounge right now is crying for blood over the K-Bot allegations. There could be a riot soon." Brya amended her flight plan to take her to Prime instead.

After that, she would make things up as she went along. She wasn't broke. She could afford to look around for a new job with a company that wasn't out to completely fuck over their employees. She would settle for being fucked over only a little.

"You planning on dropping off your boat at the Fleet's base on Prime as evidence? Save them a little time?" The controller had received her amended flight plan, and Brya heard the smile in his voice. Despite the uncertainty ahead, she couldn't hide a smile, either.

"Why not? She handles hyperspace beautifully. I'd like to take one last trip before she's confiscated."

"Fuck it, just hire someone to change her ID code and keep her. Were you one of the poor sods whose ships were sabotaged?"

"Yeah. Her name was *Rapture*." Brya activated the flight checklist, watching as each item ticked green as it scanned each function necessary to sustain life in space.

"Good boat?"

"Good for me."

"That sucks. I'm serious, you should consider just keeping that freighter. Then sue the bastards—ah, shit."

"Everything okay?" And could she get the hell off this station already?

"You're cleared, Captain. The angry mob you predicted just showed up. You should probably go before they try to set something on fire or bust into your berth and you can't depart." Her comm board pinged as the controller authorized her freighter to leave Crystal Station.

"Will you be okay?"

"Eh." Brya thought she could hear the man shrugging. "I'll be fine. This isn't the first time I've dealt with a bunch of pissed-off spacers and it won't be the last. The station's fireproof and no one onboard has any lethal weapons. I have a stunner in my pocket, if it comes to that, which I doubt. I'll be fine. Safe journey, Captain Dennir. The doors are opening in ninety seconds."

Brya fired up the freighter's engines and the dock's safety lights changed from green to red as the station computers scanned for life forms. The dock's doors yawned open. The freighter was sucked into space, and Brya left Crystal Station.

The Larsen gate she was warned about when she signed on with Renascent was shaping up to be her favorite shortcut. Brya had never been prone to space sickness, even when she first fled Ralani, and she wasn't now. The gate spit her out a short distance to her destination in Alliance space, and she checked her comm board, wanting to see what news bulletins and messages she might have missed while she was incommunicado in hyperspace.

The news about Renascent Galactic had blown up over the last couple of hours and she devoured every scrap of information the freighter computer had downloaded. There had been a riot at Renascent's moon colony base, with weapons fired from all sides, making Brya glad she decided to come to Prime instead. Gleda Naith had already issued a statement through her attorney, and a class-action fund had already been set up for employees who lost their independent freighters thanks to K-Bots. Brya made a mental note to remind herself to register as a litigant.

Her personal inbox pinged an incoming transmit, stamped with Kai's address. Her heart leaped at the signature.

Still, her fingers hovered over the Accept tab, unsure. She hadn't left him under the best of circumstances. She'd said some pretty terrible things to him. Things that, in his position, she would find unforgivable.

I lied, Kai, and I'm so sorry. I love you so much but I'm not the right woman for you.

The transmit's timestamp indicated it was sent while she was still in hyperspace. She hadn't told Kai about her plans when she left him on Ishka, but he would have access to that kind of information, especially since she had stopped trying to cover her tracks the way she did when she still worked for

Wethmore and then when she flew the *Rapture*. He would know Renascent had hired her.

She braced herself and accepted the transmit.

Kai's face filled the screen. She sighed wistfully. "Brya," he said, all business. "I'm hoping you'll get this sooner rather than later. I know about Renascent Galactic's troubles and I'm sure by now you know, too." He ran his hand through his hair, nervousness flitting across his features. "I was going to send you a message anyway, even if Renascent hadn't spent so much time and money fucking over independent captains." He turned to speak to someone off-camera. "Yeah, I know, and this is a personal transmit. Don't tell me to watch my language. You're not my CO."

A smile crept across Brya's face.

He turned back to the screen. "I did this before the news broke about Renascent, but I bought the *Rapture* from the scrapyard you sold her to."

Brya's breath caught in her throat, and she almost asked why Kai would do that before remembering it was a recording.

"I fixed her," Kai said. "Stripped out the hardware, got rid of the K-Bot, repaired her hyperspace engines, and I'm *really* hoping you'll take her off my hands as soon as possible, especially given Renascent's legal troubles. I've left her at the civilian docks at the Fleet outpost on Prime Two." His expression softened. "Please get in touch when you get this. I'm not mad at you, I'm not trying to run your life. You know how I feel and that hasn't changed. I care about you, Brya."

He paused, then gave a small wave to the camera before the transmit ended.

Brya burst into tears.

Noisy sobs escaped her as she keyed in a course for Prime Two, not caring that it deviated from her original flight plan. She doubted that the transit controller at Crystal Station or anyone at Renascent cared about a tiny diversion from an empty freighter, anyway.

Kai's feelings hadn't changed. She was surprised, grateful, and humbled to know that, and she had no idea how anything could work between them, but maybe it was worth a shot.

She wiped her eyes and blew her nose, cleaning herself up as best as she could, before launching a transmit to record.

"Kai," she began, "You didn't have to do this."

CHAPTER 13

Kai waited at Prime Two's civilian docks, pacing the length of the corridor. Where was she?

Soon, he reminded himself. *She said she was only an hour out in her transmit, she'll be here soon, she won't run away this time...*

At least, he hoped she wouldn't run away this time.

The whoosh of doors cycling at the end of the corridor had his heart racing, and he looked in that direction. He spotted a mop of familiar multicolored hair. Beneath it was Brya, wearing a new-looking gray shipsuit bearing Renascent Galactic patches.

She saw him and started running. Kai remained rooted to the spot until Brya unexpectedly threw her arms around him in a fierce hug he hadn't dared to hope for. "Thank you," she said in his ear.

His arms wrapped around her, not wanting to let go. "I'd do anything for you."

She sniffled. "I don't know why."

"Because I love you, Brya." He'd said it before and he would keep telling her until she believed him.

"I love you, too."

He was struck speechless at that admission, hardly daring to believe he'd really heard it.

She pulled away enough to face him. Tears filled her eyes. "I'm sorry," she said. "These last weeks have been so miserable for me, and I've missed you so much. I thought you deserved someone better." She pulled away from him so they could face each other. "I fucked up everything so badly ever since we left Ralani. I always do. I wrecked my life and I didn't want to wreck yours."

"I don't care about that."

"I know that now. And I'm still scared I'm going to do something to destroy your life or career. It's sort of my specialty."

"It isn't. You're a lot more resourceful and intelligent than you think. You're always going to be okay, Brya."

Her aura glowed, a sure sign of happiness. It contradicted how her body trembled in his arms. "I don't know how to make this work."

"We'll figure it out." He let her go and laced his fingers through hers. "Want to see the *Rapture*?"

She sucked in a deep breath, as though trying to quell the flutters in her stomach. "I still can't believe you did that."

He led her to the berth doors and palmed open the lock. They were met with a rush of cold air, but neither of them noticed as Brya gasped at the sight of the freighter. "She's totally bot-free and fully operational," Kai said as Brya rushed to her ship. The lock still recognized her handprint and she launched the cargo bay's ramp. He followed her into the ship's belly.

She turned around, gazing at the empty bay as if seeing it for the first time. "It's your ship but better," he said.

"It's... Kai, this is the best thing that anyone's ever done for me."

Warmth spread through him at her words. "There's

something else." He didn't want to blow his own horn, but he'd rather tell her how the K-Bot investigation started himself. "This hasn't been made public yet, but I launched the K-Bot investigation into Renascent."

She froze, mouth open in an "O" of shock. "That was you?"

"Well, Lieutenant Anders helped. You met him on Ishka when he shot Wethmore. It seemed weird that a K-Bot would be installed on a ship like yours. We did some cross-referencing with invasive malware reports aboard independent freighters and Renascent Galactic was the common denominator. That information will probably go public in the next couple of days, including stuff about the *Rapture*."

"So you're giving me a heads up about a possible media frenzy?"

"Exactly."

"Maybe I'll be in hyperspace by then and won't have to take questions from reporters." But she didn't seem put out about it. She wasn't even really paying attention to the *Rapture* anymore and had crossed the cargo bay to Kai, taking his hand again.

"Yeah, no more two-week trips through space."

"I can't believe you did all of this."

"I want you to be happy, Brya. I've always wanted that."

They walked through the *Rapture*'s corridors, still unchanged, but empty of furniture and fixtures that Brya had been forced to sell along with the ship herself. "There's something else," Kai said. "My contract with the Fleet is up for renewal in six weeks. I'm not renewing it. I'm going into the independent shipping business with you."

Her eyes widened with alarm. "But your career!"

"It doesn't mean anything to me if I can't be with you. I told you before, I spent years looking for you. I'm not passing on a chance to spend the rest of my life with you again."

They stopped at the cockpit. The computers were dark, but Brya activated them, and they both looked at the ship's systems activating with delight. "You really want to do this?" she asked.

"I really want to do this with you." He sat down in the captain's chair and pulled her down into his lap.

"Can *I* sit in the captain's chair?"

"You can sit wherever you want."

She snuggled against his chest. "I can't wait to start flying her again." She craned her face up to meet his, lips meeting a in a fierce kiss.

The small motion was enough to evoke powerful memories of the last time they'd kissed on the *Rapture* and what that led to, and his regret that there wasn't any furniture in the captain's quarters. She shifted until she straddled his lap and wrapped her arms around his neck. "Remember what you said about the wall?" She blushed.

"Remember what *you* said about foreplay?" He paused. "Maybe that was me."

"Does it matter?"

"No," he said. "We'll use the captain's seat. It still needs to be broken in."

A giggle escaped her, and she sank against him. "Kai, I can't believe you still want to be with me," she said, gaze fixing on his. Her mirth evaporated and her next words were serious. "I didn't think I was worthy of you."

"You are. You always were." He would never stop reminding her of that.

She shook her head slightly. "I fucked up a lot, I know that. I didn't want to push you away. I thought I *had* to. I thought you were better off without me."

He knew that, and it still tore at him that she felt that way. "No," he said. "My life is better with you in it."

"I love you, Kai," she said.

Those words would never fail to send a thrill through him. "Tell me again."

"Kai," she said deliberately, fingers resting against his jaw. "I love you. I'll never leave you again."

"I love you, too." He eased them off the control panel. "There's just one more thing this ship needs."

"A new bed?"

"Exactly." He kissed her, relishing the contact, knowing he'd never get enough of her. "A bed, and everything that makes this ship a home."

"Kai," she said, "I don't care about that. Anywhere you are —that's my home."

ABOUT THE AUTHOR

Jessica Marting is a sci-fi and paranormal romance author, art enthusiast (not quite an artist, despite all that time in art school), an avid reader, and makeup collector. She lives in Toronto.

Sign up for her newsletter at jessicamarting.com/newsletter for pre-order alerts, sales, freebies, and more.

ALSO BY JESSICA MARTING

Magic & Mechanicals

Wolf's Lady

Sea Change

Bound in Blood

Dragon's Keep

Spellbound

Zone Cyborgs

Haven

Paradise

Oasis

Safe Harbor

Sanctuary

Refuge

The Commons

Supernova

Celestial Chaos

Standalone Novels & Novellas

Spindle's End

Trade Secrets

Neon Vice

Dead Ringer